HATE HIM

A PSYCHOLOGICAL THRILLER ROMANCE

SIN AND INNOCENCE
BOOK TWO

VIOLET HAZE

STOKED PUBLISHING HOUSE

Hate Him (Sin and Innocence Part Two)
©2025 by Violet Haze

This is a work of fiction. Names, characters, places, and incidents are the product of the author's imagination or are used fictitiously. Any resemblance to actual persons, living or dead, events, or locales is entirely coincidental.

Cover from Designs by Dana
Stoked Publishing House
ISBN-13: 978-1-7355302-5-3
First Edition: September 2025

DISCLAIMER

Part Two of this **dark psychological thriller romance** story contains scenes of potentially triggering mature content one may find disturbing. If this book were a movie, it would be Rated R.

Please do not proceed if uncomfortable consuming this kind of content. The author doesn't condone any bad actions taken by any character in this *fictional* novel.

1

MADDIE

Where is the door?
I blink into the darkness, my brow
    furrowing as trees surround me
    instead of walls, and a slight
    breeze wafts across my skin.
What the hell?
Then I'm falling.
Screaming.
Flailing as I land in water, sinking
    to the bottom.
Only something clings to the bottom
    of my leg, holding me down and
    keeping me from getting back
    up to the surface.
Antosha's face fills my sights as he
    grabs my arms, tugging on me
    and frowning as my body won't

*move no matter how hard he
yanks. I'm afraid he'll tear them
off and I struggle, crying out as
it's now Gaspard's face blocking
my vision.
Crying. Crying tears at the bottom
of the water, until I gag.
I'm choking, coughing, sputtering.
Oh, god, I'm going to die,
and there's nothing I can do
about that.
My life is over.*

I JOLT AWAKE, GASPING FOR AIR AS MY HANDS fly to my throat. My breath is heavy and ragged as I try to make sense of my surroundings in the dim light.

Light!

I blink once, twice, unable to believe the sight before my eyes.

I'm no longer in the cramped box he trapped me in for what felt like eternity. Instead, I'm in a familiar room—my bedroom in Gaspard's house. In the four poster bed with its luxurious silk sheets and equally lush down comforter. The walls are lined with emerald green wallpaper and the curtains match in color, elegantly framing the large windows. The carpet is plush and white, making me want to kick off my shoes and sink into its softness.

But this is all just a facade of luxury; I'm in a bed I hate in a room I despise, all in the house owned by a man who makes my skin crawl.

A man I can't wait to kill if ever given the chance.

Whoa!

Where did that thought come from?

I've never been a violent person. Perhaps that is a bad thing considering all he's put me through, but I can't imagine taking another's life, despite how much I would enjoy watching the life drain from his eyes.

Oh... wow.

Fuck.

I shove a hand through my hair and toss the heavy blankets off me. I must've been in that box for way too long if my thoughts are turning murderous and gleeful at the thought of killing Gaspard.

He is a disgusting human being. One who tortures me more by keeping me in some stupid ass box and only feeding me while keeping me in relative darkness.

Everything is about control with him, about making sure I understand he's in charge and I never will be. That he owns me down to the bone and always will; nobody is coming to save me and he showed me that no matter where I run... he will find me.

The baby kicks, knocking me out of my thoughts. I rub my stomach to let her know everything will be okay, although if I'm not sure if that's true. I have to remain calm; she tends to kick more if I'm upset or anxious or start to worry. It's like she's aware I need to stay focused and helps me remain steady despite the current situation.

Pushing myself off the high bed, I stand on shaky legs and face the looming figure of Gaspard standing at the door. His deep voice breaks through the silence, commenting on my appearance with words that make my blood boil.

"You are glowing, *ma souris*."

Mouse. The nickname he gave me years ago, when he first took control of my life. He always finds twisted ways to compliment or insult me, reminding me that he owns me and will never let me go.

But I can't show any fear or weakness in front of him, not when I have to protect my child. So I stand tall and steady as he stalks toward me, trying to hide the shaking in my hands as I scoff at his comment.

"No thanks to you!" The words escape before I

think better about what flies out of my mouth around him, sucking in a breath as he stalks toward me.

My false bravado doesn't stop me from whimpering as he stops in front of me and grabs my face, squeezing my cheeks tight as he lowers his voice. His hold contains a controlled rage I've no desire to experience the full pain of ever again. "Your little adventure has made you bold, hm? You dare to speak to me in such a way after the trouble you caused?"

He doesn't release his grip because he doesn't care for a reply as he continues on, his eyes now slits a mix of suppressed rage and desire I've come to dread. "You would dare to try and take the child from me, after everything I provided for you and your mother. My child, *salope*. And to live with those men? You are mine. Do you understand?"

I wince at the familiar insults he hurls at me, the ones he reserves for when he's truly furious. But this time, his tone has shifted into something dark and twisted that makes my stomach churn.

He's always been evil, ever since we moved into his house years ago. But now it's clear that he's not just evil, he's sick and perverse too. And if I try to leave him again... I don't want to think about what he'll do, which doesn't matter because his next words chill me from the inside out.

"I will not be disobeyed. You will stay. Hm? Unless you wish for your new friends to meet their maker."

My stomach roils at the thought of Gaspard torturing and killing the Valiquette men. I'm not sure he'll actually do it; hell, I'm no longer certain about what he is capable of or how far he's willing to go to keep me with him.

But one thing is certain: I am trapped here with him, no matter how much I might resist.

I am his, heart and soul, whether I want to be or not.

He releases my face and straightens, towering over me once more, his voice dripping with malice. "Understand, *ma souris*? You will not disobey me or leave again. If you do, your friends will bear the consequences."

I nod as he moves to grab my face again, stuttering over the hated words I haven't had to say since I left, terrified to say anything else that might set him off. "Y—yes, Sir."

"Good."

His gaze flicks down to my stomach and his face lights up with a smile that makes my blood run cold. It's the same smile Antosha had upon witnessing the sonogram of the baby, but this is Gaspard. The thought of him touching me, wanting me to bear his child, makes my stomach twist in disgust.

"I hear we are expecting a girl." His voice is suddenly sickly sweet. "It isn't the son I desire, but we will try again, hm?"

Oh, god.

My mind reels at the thought of having another child with this sick man. This isn't something I ever wanted or agreed to. I manage to keep my face neutral despite my desire to scream about how he'll never touch me again, so no, we won't be having a fucking son.

Not that I trick him for a moment.

His smirk is back, eyes darkening as his mood changes. He lifts his hand to my cheek and strokes with the pad of his thumb, shaking his head and clicking his tongue as his tone darkens once again. His smile is cruel as he sneers, "You never were one for hiding your thoughts, *ma souris*. Remember your friends. I waited for the perfect moment this time. I won't be so kind if you run again."

My heart pounds as he leans in, presses a soft kiss to my dry lips, and then leaves the room without another word. I try not to heave at the sudden lurch of my stomach from his touch.

I'm glad my companion who has always assisted me is close by as he walks out the door because my knees buckle under me, tears streaming down my cheeks. She reaches me seconds before I hit the ground and helps me over to the bed.

"Maddie, you must breathe." Eva separates my knees and nods as my watery eyes meets her. "Lowering your head between your legs will help with the panic."

Doubt it, but I do what she says to the best of my ability, one hand on my belly as I try to comfort myself and my baby.

Then, as she always done while I lived here, she tells me everything I need to know as she lowers her voice.

"I'm sorry, Maddie. I tried to hold him off as long as possible before he sent out notices that you were missing. You know how he is." Her voices wobbles and I don't need to look up at her to know she's as close to tears as ever. "He said he would hurt my family."

Yes, that's what he does.

He'll threaten to harm others if you don't tell him what he wants to know. I've never found out he's actually hurt anyone, but this is the first time I've crossed him.

Not that Eva would be aware of him hurting her family or not unless he wanted to gloat about it. Once you take work in this household, you sign a contract and you can't leave for a predetermined amount of years. It's amazing the amount of power

Gaspard has to make such contracts legally binding, including one that prohibits a person from sharing anything that goes on in the house. Break the NDA, face fines and potential jail time because he has *that* much power indeed.

"I understand, Eva. You tried your best." I take a deep breath and with a hand to my chest, I lift my head to meet her gaze. "Thank you."

She helped me leave and risked a lot to do so, as well as to distract him for a few days by telling him I was violently ill.

If there's anything Gaspard can't stand being around, it's vomit, and it had been easy to do that enough to trick him enough for me to escape.

"I don't know how you can run away again, Maddie. He's tightened security to the point I can't go out without an escort. All ways out of the house have someone guarding it as well."

"I'm not surprised. We knew it was a one shot kind of thing."

"I'm sorry." She sniffles, glancing down at my stomach and shaking her head. "This is wrong. You and the baby don't deserve to have to live with such a monster as that man. If only I could have done more."

"You did everything right, Eva. I shouldn't have gone outside, no matter how nice the weather. But he would've found a way. If not then, another day." At that thought, I clear my throat and run a hand through my hair. "How long was I in that box or whatever?"

"Cage." She looks incredibly guilty as she says, "Three days."

Holy hell.

Three days.

He wanted to teach me a lesson and show me what things will be like if I dare to leave him again.

If I dare to defy him, to try and take away what he considers belongs to him.

Me. Our unborn daughter.

His grasp is tight, strict, and far reaching.

He'll punish me if I don't do as he asks. And now that I came of age while living with the Valiquette men, he'll rush to marry me and put the final nail in the coffin of my life. He doesn't care about what I want or need. That I don't want him or this life.

The moment he mentioned hurting the Valiquette men, though, my defiance cracked, because he isn't one to bluff. He will go to any length to prevent me from relying on anyone except him.

Gaspard is the center of the universe in his world. This is his house, his city, and I am his and his alone.

I'm never going to get away. Not until he's dead.

And perhaps I should kill him. I've thought about it many times. But if life as his wife is anything similar to before I ran away, then there is little chance or opportunity for me to get my hands on something to commit the crime with.

I'm sad. Terrified.

Almost positive I'll never escape from beneath his thumb. Nor will my daughter or any other children he wishes to have despite what I want.

And Eva is as trapped as I am.

Never have I wanted to scream and cry as much as I do right now.

"Maddie." Eva drops to her knees as I close my eyes, attempting to withhold those feelings from manifesting, and wraps her arms around me. "I will do whatever I can to help you get out of here again. I swear it."

Swiping at the tears dripping down my face, I shake my head while returning her embrace. "You can't. We must do as he says. I will not see anyone else suffer at his hands. Not if I can prevent it."

"But Maddie—"

Pulling back, my smile is sad. "No, Eva. I tried and failed. We must give in. I don't wish for him to harm you, especially since you assisted me in leaving the first time. He'll be watching us too closely now."

She stares at me, pondering whether I've truly given up, and she must see the something in my eyes I'm unable to hide — complete and utter despair.

Lowering her own gaze, she nods before rising to her feet. "You're right. Do you need anything else?"

"No, thank you, Eva."

As she exits the room, I curl into a ball on my bed. With nothing I can do except cry my eyes out until zero tears are left, I'm alone and forced to face my new reality with an ice cold wall around my heart.

MADDIE

After the press conference announcing my return ends, Gaspard leads me into his office and pushes me down into the chair across from his.

"You did well. Your obedience today pleased me, *ma souris*."

My obedience. Right.

Like the fact I wore the heaviest coat I own — at his request — in order to hide the pregnancy from the eyes of the media. He doesn't want anyone to know what he's done. I considered allowing my coat to float open in the cool breeze out there, but the fact he held my hand tight enough to hurt the entire time kept me in line.

And this ring on my finger? Big, ugly, and the weight of the metal bothers me more than only in the physical manner.

He might as well place a rope around my neck

because every moment in this house with this ring on my hand makes me feel like I'm being choked to death.

I don't respond to him. Most of the time it isn't necessary because he doesn't care what I think or feel. To him, I'm nothing more than a possession, a thing for him to use as he sees fit.

A fact he reminds me of each time his mouth opens, like now as he announces, "We will marry tomorrow."

Tomorrow?

My stomach roils, my heart jumping into my throat at the thought of being tied to this man legally.

I want to scream, to get up out of this chair and run, but I can't. My entire body feels weighed down by his threats of harm against me and anyone I care about.

Since the day he promised to harm the Valiquette men, I've tried not to think about them at all. Especially Antosha. There's a constant ache in my chest as I miss him so much and there's nothing I can do to change anything without considerable risk to him and Guillame.

Both of them might not care or may want me to fight despite whether doing so puts them in danger. I don't know if I'm good with that, though. I'm hesitant to talk about trying to escape again with

Eva, wondering if Gaspard is listening to all the conversation in this house.

I told her there wasn't anything to do except what he says, to not try to leave because I don't want him to anyone else, but what else was I supposed to say? I'm not sure I'll get another chance to run — and once I have the baby, escaping will become harder, if not nearly impossible.

There's zero chance in hell I'll leave my daughter behind with this monster.

I'll die trying first.

"Pay attention!"

He startles me out of my thoughts and it's hard not to flinch at his presence in front of me. He crouches down, puts his hands on my shoulder, and smiles as if we're nothing more than an average couple.

It takes every ounce of self-control I have to not flinch when he moves one hand to push some hair behind my hair and then cups my cheek. I close my eyes; not to savor the feel of his thumb caressing my cheek, but to avoid allowing him to see any of my emotions about this situation.

The desire to push him away intensifies as he leans in closer, his hot breath reaching my lips seconds before his mouth touches mine. I try not to react, to avoid thinking about how he's the last person in the world I want kissing me, but he's smart enough to know what I'm doing.

He sighs, the sound filled with disappointment and irritation, before firming his grasp on my face to shove his tongue in my mouth.

My whimper is swallowed up as my hands automatically come up in an attempt to push him away. His hand moves into my hair and he grips a handful in his fist, yanking hard enough to cause tears to spring up and my eyes to fly open.

God, I hate him. I don't want him to touch me, to do any of this to me, and the last thing I want is to marry him. Pure emotional reaction takes over. All logic about trying to keep others safe is gone as I lash out, my hands smacking against his shoulders the longer he tries to take what he wants.

When he releases me, the action is almost the same as if he dropped me to the ground, which makes me glad I'm sitting down. He lets go all at once with a growl of anger, which is only interrupted by the sound of his phone ringing.

"Get out," he barks at me without looking in my direction. "We will talk about this later."

I don't need him to tell me twice. Scrambling up out of the chair, I practically run out of the room, sighing with relief with the door slams closed behind me.

Although there isn't any real relief in sight.

He'll make me pay for my reaction at some point in the future, near or far. Whatever and whenever works for him, perhaps when I least expect it. Well, he might think I won't expect it, but I am always on guard around him.

Around everyone in this house, except for Eva. It is exhausting to have little privacy and to watch everything I say, especially with her. She's the only person I trust in this house but I fear retaliation against us both were either of us to speak of anything except the most boring of topics.

Before and now, my life here is lonely. There isn't much to do besides read or walk aimlessly around the house. I am allowed out in the garden but there isn't much joy in being watched closely by two guards who are sure to report the slightest offense to Gaspard.

I don't speak to most of the staff. There are quite a few of them who choose to work for him — they aren't tied down from fear like Eva and many of the others like her. The guards, especially, are paid well to look the other way.

I hate that as I head toward my bedroom, I can feel their eyes on me, their gaze following my trek down the hallway and up the stairs.

I am not in a home; this place is nothing more than a prison.

And my daughter doesn't deserve to grow up in this environment.

I don't deserve his treatment either or to be held against my will, and because nobody—such as Eva—despite what she agreed to upon taking a job in this household, deserves to have a proverbial knife at their throat for years on end.

And somehow, I must find a way to escape again, even in the face of the consequences he has threatened me with because to stay here is quickly becoming a fate worse than death for all us suffering beneath the weight of his cruelty.

3

MADDIE

Marrying Gaspard involves little more than signing my name as he watches me closely, followed by him slipping a second ring on my finger and kissing my lips once.

Afterward, he shoos me away as if I'm bothering him, and promises to see me later in the evening.

There isn't much to care about here. I've only been grateful for the fact he hasn't forced me to come back to his bed and believe my pregnancy is the reason. Outside of his harsh attitude toward me, he has been gentler than before and I appreciate it. Not that I forgive him for what he's done and continues doing to me.

It's been getting warmer outside, and I feel like my stomach gets bigger by the minute. Although every kick and movement of my baby brings a smile to my face, I'm uncomfortable most of the time. It's hard to sleep — no position is comfortable, no matter how many pillows I use for support.

So instead of sleeping, my time in bed is the only moments where I allow myself to think about Antosha. About how kind he was and the way he... touched me the night before my abduction and return to hell.

That stolen time together is something I've kept to myself, something I haven't told Eva either. Not because I think she would say anything bad about what happened; more that the less anyone knows about what happened between us, the better. Especially in this house.

I don't want her to have information he could potentially get from her using his evil and manipulative ways. Knowing I allowed Antosha to touch me would probably result in him doing what he threatened to do if I attempt to leave again.

But fuck... Every time those memories enter my mind, it's hard to ignore the way my body reacts. My skin heats, I'm instantly aroused, and the slightest touch from my own hands isn't enough to alleviate the need that flows through me because my body wants him.

I love it but also hate it. The way my body acts like there's a need for him after only one time, especially when I'll probably never see him again. I don't cry and it takes everything I have to not miss him, to not hope for some miracle.

To not think about what I'll never have again.

And Eva, always perceptive of when my mood changes, tries to distract from my becoming Gaspard's wife when I enter my room a little bit later as she asks, "What would you like to do?"

"I don't know." Walking over to the comfy chair by the window, I sink into it with a sigh. "Not much to do, as usual."

"Boredom will make you crazy," she responds, laughing softly, although the sound isn't joyful. "We must try to stay occupied."

I know she's right. Eva is technically a maid — she's responsible for keeping my areas clean, although I do my best to keep her from having much to do in that regard. However, she's also my companion as well, and apparently was tasked by Gaspard to do more to keep me occupied upon my return.

I don't know how he expects her to do that. Hell, how he expects me to always be doing something when there isn't much here for me to do.

And yes, I am bored out of my mind, and mostly joking when I say, "We can play some chess if you can find a set in this house."

Eva's eyebrows almost fly through the roof as

her lips quirk with a suppressed laugh. "Chess? Do you know how to play?"

"I do." Not that I will tell her how that's come about, but she understands anyway, if her excited expression is anything to go by. "And I'll teach you, if you want."

I love the way her whole face brightens at the idea as she nods. "I will see what I can find."

"Okay."

After she leaves the room, I get up and get some comfortable clothes for the evening, then head into the bathroom to shower.

I'm not alone for more than a few minutes before the door creaks open and I call out, "Did you find one, Eva?"

"If you wanted to play chess," Gaspard's deep voice answers, "all you had to do was ask."

I turn around with a gasp as the door slides open and he sticks his head in, chuckling. I use one hand to cover my breasts before realizing the futility of that action as they've gotten too big for my arm to cover.

A fact he uses to his advantage while gazing at me, all his focus on how what he's done has changed my body.

I want to speak, but I don't know what to say. He's close enough to touch me and when he finally reaches out, I shudder from the pure revulsion everything about him makes me feel.

As his hand lands on my stomach, I flinch, hating his touch with everything in me and despising the pure glee on his face at the result of his actions.

I want to cry and scream and push him away, yet I'm frozen in place, barely able to breathe as the hot water beats on my back.

And only when he finally takes his hand away do I take a deep breath. Using all of my control to keep the tears in my eyes from escaping, I whisper, "I need to finish showering."

He smiles. "Of course." Before stepping back, he adds, "Until later, *ma souris*."

I don't know if that's a promise for this evening or not, but I'm determined to spend as little time with him as possible. After quickly washing up, I dry off and dress, then see Eva putting down the chess board on the table as I return to my bedroom.

She looks up as I approach, expression switching from panic to relief. "There you are! How do we set it up?"

"I'll show you."

We sink into the plush chairs, settling in for the first game. Eva's slender fingers pick up a piece and she turns it over in her hand, examining it curiously.

"So... we each have eight pieces and the objective is to move them to the other side?" she asks.

I nod, explaining the rules before asking, "Understood?"

"Absolutely. Let's play!"

Eva is determined and honestly, it's nice to see her smile for once. Makes me glad I suggested we do this if only to help pass time.

We take a few minutes to survey the pieces on the board, strategizing our moves before Eva places her pawn down on the first row and advances it two squares.

"Is this how it's played?"

"Yes," I respond while making my first move.

And with that, the game officially begins.

"The pawns are called foot soldiers," I tell her after a few moments, explaining things to her the way Guillame did for me. "Representing the weakest piece on the board, like infantry compared to knights and queens."

"That's interesting," Eva muses. "But can't they also be promoted to any other piece if they reach the other side?"

I nod. "Exactly. Though they may start off as the weakest, pawns have potential to become the strongest piece if utilized correctly."

Eva nods thoughtfully. I can sense her mind

working, perhaps not only about the intricacies of chess but also about my current situation. We both know we can't openly discuss anything involving escape; it would put both of us in danger. But there is an unspoken understanding between us now — we are both smarter and more determined since my capture and return. I don't know if I'll ever get out of here again, but if I do, I won't leave Eva behind. She doesn't deserve Gaspard's cruelty any more than I do.

The game continues for some time until I ultimately win. But I can see that Eva is getting better with each move; a fast learner with unwavering perseverance.

"How about another round?"

She grins confidently at my suggestion. "Absolutely. And this time, I will win."

I raise an eyebrow in amusement. "You're on."

But despite her conviction, she doesn't win.

"You are quite skilled at this game," Eva compliments me while laughing. She gazes at me curiously, but for once, I can't decipher her thoughts.

"Thank you," I reply with a small smile. Maybe she wants to ask me who taught me how to play chess in the short time I was gone, but I don't want to think about Antosha or Guillame right now. Glancing at the clock, I realize how late it is and let out a heavy sigh. "I suppose I should retire for the night."

Because she knows how strict Gaspard is about my bedtime, she nods quietly, the smile slipping from her face as she cleans up the game and wishes me goodnight.

And as I slip into bed, after feeling peaceful for the last few hours while playing the game with Eva, I'm all too aware the peace won't last long and that the only way to get through this hell is to make sure he has no clue about the plans I'll have to make to break us free once and for all.

4

ANTOSHA

The place is a fortress.

Both my uncle and Léonie believe I am out dealing with business and it is best they continue to believe this until I'm certain of the next course of action to take.

However, as much as I've gotten original building plans of the house, I am certain there have been changes in the many years Malveaux has owned it and the land it occupies.

A tall iron-wrought fence with pointed tips surrounds the property around every inch and there is little chance of getting through the main gate without an invitation.

Things appear as if the man considered every angle of his ability to trap people long before his actual rise to power. His meticulous planning makes me wonder about his original intentions in dating and marrying Madeline's mother, my concerns leading to a quiet investigation into the records of her death.

I don't expect it will bear much fruit. If he had any hand in her death, he would've done well to cover his tracks, and my true purpose is nothing more than to free Madeline from his grasp forever.

The problem is there doesn't appear any way to contact her, nor to get into the house. Not many people come or go from the house and those that do are mainly guards or those who have Malveaux's confidence.

I've considered abducting one of them, to make them talk about how to get into the house to retrieve her, but have enough intelligence to know the only repercussions will be against Madeline if he believes her in on the operation.

Five weeks have passed since the news conference spreading the word about her return and he has certainly married her by now. She will be due not long from now and every day I fear for her safety as well as the child's.

A man like him isn't afraid of consequences, of doing whatever it takes to keep someone in his control. No one has dared to cross the man in years and his re-election has been nothing more than a campaign of a cunning man capable of fooling many into believing he's a good person.

Although I have questioned how he will explain the presence of a child, that may not be a concern of his as the plan might simply be to never let the child into the public's view.

It is disgraceful that Madeline will live a life of loneliness; one where what should be the joy of motherhood is overshadowed by how her children will arrive in this world.

I fear never again seeing her smile, hearing her laughter, or the feel of her soft lips against mine. As the days have passed, I think about her more, wanting to hold her in my arms and give her comfort. I want to tell her she's safe and will never have to deal with him again.

The only issue is how to make that happen when Malveaux is one of the most well-guarded men in the city. For the last few weeks, when the opportunity arose, I have observed the house as well as all activity coming and going in hopes of finding a crack to exploit.

A disappointing venture up to this point.

And as the sky grows dark, I head home, determined as ever to find a way to free her, no matter the cost.

"You were gone quite a while," Léonie comments from behind me several days later, her hands landing softly on my shoulders. "Everything good?"

"Yes."

She sighs, sitting next to me and placing a hand on my thigh as she shakes her head. "You're hiding something."

I don't respond. She has been fishing for information for weeks and I refuse to confirm her suspicions.

"Antosha, it is rude to ignore me."

"I am not ignoring you. I'm thinking."

She pauses, then asks softly, "About the girl?"

Her question confirms it was stupid to assume she wouldn't find out what I've been up to. Léonie has always been a highly intelligent woman and she doesn't put up with anyone's bullshit — including mine.

"It is impossible to not think about her."

"Only because you refuse to let her go." She removes her hand from my thigh and releases a heavy, exasperated breath. "What can you do for the girl, Antosha? You must acknowledge she is out of your reach."

"I promised her she wouldn't have to go back there. I'm not the type of man to let someone remain in a bad situation because providing help appears impossible. You wouldn't have married such a man."

Another sigh as she nods. "You're right. I am not ignorant of what you've been up to. Surely you must have an idea in mind?"

"I've examined every angle of the house and have watched for weeks. There is no way to get inside or get a message to her."

Familiar with her expressions, the newest one tells me she wants to say she told me so, though she won't. She merely sits beside me, quiet and waiting for me to have a brilliant idea to move forward with my insistence on helping Madeline.

But although I don't wish to admit anything out loud to her or my uncle, the situation is looking more hopeless by the day, despite my determination otherwise.

When she finally speaks, it's to change the topic and fill the silence. "We need to focus on our life together, Antosha. Our marriage. Having a child. Our families expect it."

Not a conversation I want to have at this time.... or perhaps forever. "When the time is right—"

"No." She moves swiftly until she's straddling my lap and glares down at me, her hands once again resting on my shoulders. "I have had enough of this. You haven't touched me and it has been months since our wedding. I am your wife."

"Léonie—"

"Touch me," she pleads, sliding her hands down to the center of my chest. "Don't make me beg."

There is nothing I can say to her in this situation. I remain silent as she does her best to entice me, leaning in to press her lips against mine while undoing the buttons on my shirt, one by one.

It doesn't matter that I am not the one she wants, nor is she the one I want. She whimpers when I respond to her kiss with the barest one in return, growling in frustration and taking my shirt in her fists. "Pretend I'm her, Antosha. I don't care. We must do this."

Léonie is nothing if not a dutiful daughter. It is true that our duty is to create a family, to strengthen the bonds of our families uniting by having children, and there is no stopping her commitment to fulfill what she feels is her responsibility.

Before Maddie, that responsibility weighed heavily upon my shoulders as well, but as this beautiful, captivating woman begs for my touch, there is no comparing the two women.

There is one woman I want and my wife isn't her—a fact no amount of pretending will fix.

And Léonie... my strong, passionate, dutiful friend... realizes this fact with the saddest expression I've ever seen cross her face. As her eyes well with tears, she leans into me, resting her face against my chest as her shoulders shake while giving into the emotions she can no longer hold back.

"I'm sorry." I kiss the top of her head, wrapping my arms around her as she sobs. "Please forgive me."

Fuck knows it will be a long time before I forgive myself for hurting the one person who has always been there for me. When she finally lifts her head and dries her eyes, though, she lets me know she's on my side with four simple words.

"Let's get the bastard."

5

———

MADDIE

As I'm helping clean up after another game of chess a few nights later, Eva whispers to me, "I've got a plan to get you out of here."

I stare at her in confusion, and she clarifies, "It's wrong that nobody here does anything about what he's doing to you. I couldn't stand it before and that hasn't changed."

"It's too dangerous."

"Staying here will be worse. We both know that," she replies as a piece drops to the floor. "Tell me their names."

She wants to know the names of the men who helped me, but I don't understand why she needs to know; it's not like she can contact them. I'll tell her anyway though because what difference does it make?

I hate the fact I can't talk freely without

worrying about Gaspard listening in. I've searched my room for any evidence of listening devices, but I haven't found any. Eva crouches to pick up the piece that fell on the floor, and as she straightens up, I whisper Antosha's full name to her.

Her eyes widen and she smiles. It's the biggest smile I've ever seen on her face as she whispers, "Oh my god, I know him."

"What?" Her answer surprises me. "How?"

"I mean, I know of him and his uncle. They are good people," she says in a low voice. She puts the piece with the others and closes the chess box before saying in her normal tone and volume of voice, "Do you need anything else before I go?"

I want to ask her how she knows about them and what she knows exactly, needing to understand how she knows what kind of people they are. And most of all, I want to know what her plan is to get me out of here.

But I can't ask her any of these questions right now because as always, I need to be in bed at a certain time. Gaspard says it's good for me to get regular sleep, as if I'm not an adult who can determine my own bedtime, and I'm starting to get angry at being treated like a child. I may not want to be his wife, but if he's going to expect me to do so, why is it too much to ask that he treats me like an adult with a brain?

I don't tell her any of that or ask any further questions because for now, there's nothing I can do except get rest. So I say, "No, thank you."

"All right. Trust me, Maddie. And sleep well, friend," Eva whispers, winking at me before she turns and leaves the room.

I do trust her, but I don't want Gaspard to hurt her. She is a good person and helping me isn't worth her life. I may not want to be here, but I don't want anyone else to suffer because of my situation.

As I lie in bed that night, the thought of freedom keeps me going. I remain determined to find a way out of this place because there is so much more to life than being Gaspard's prisoner and broodmare.

THE NEXT DAY, GASPARD TREATS ME WORSE than usual. After sending Eva to tell me to meet him in his office, he towers over me, all pretense of the civility he displays in front of others gone as he says, "You are disrespectful, *ma souris*."

"Disrespectful?" My heart pounds as I try to figure out what he's talking about. All I've done is spend time with Eva playing chess, trying to stay out of his way and say nothing to anger him. My eyes drops as I whisper, "I'm sorry, for whatever I did. I'm trying..."

"Speak up." He grabs my face, forcing me to look at him. "You are my wife. You need to accept your place and act loving as a wife should."

Tears fall from my eyes because there's no way I can pretend to love this awful man. I stand there in silence, waiting for him to tell me what he wants. Guessing will only lead to me feeling more and more like there's nothing I can do right.

"Tonight," he sneers as his hand slides down to my neck in a threatening manner, "you will join me in my bed and sleep there moving forward. You will be obedient and not complain or whine any more about your duties. Am I understood?"

"Yes, Sir." I say through the tears, the pain of him squeezing my throat enough to send chills through me. What other choice do I have? "I understand."

"See that you do, *ma souris*. I have given you time, but my patience with you has ended."

With those words, he covers my lips with his and forces his tongue inside. It takes every bit of my focus to soften in his arms and open up for the invasion. He must be pleased as he moans and wraps his arms around my body, and I'm only thankful for the fact he's no longer slightly strangling me. His grip tightens though, when his tongue tries to tangle with mine and I don't respond instantly. I cry out into his mouth as his fingers dig into my back and reluctantly engage in a deeper kiss.

I hate every second of it. Each day that passes makes it harder to remember how it felt to kiss Antosha and now, the disgusting taste of cigars fills my mouth instead. Gaspard prolongs the kiss as long as possible, until I'm limp in his arms and kissing him back mechanically to avoid any further punishment.

Suddenly, he ends the kiss with a hiss, his hand back around my neck as he growls, "Wraps your arms around me, *ma souris*. You are my wife, you must touch me as I touch you."

Tears prick my eyes. "Please," I beg him softly, hoping to avoid any further attention from him and having to pretend I want him to violate me. "I feel sick and want to lay down."

His grip tightens to the point I gasp, unable to breathe as he snaps at me. "You will do as you are told, *ma souris*. Now, wrap your arms around me and show me the affection a wife gives her husband."

The room spins as I struggle to suck in air and he waits expectantly. I've gone too far and he's going to choke me to death if I don't do as he says. I can't believe he would harm me when I'm pregnant with his child, but it is clear he cares more about controlling and humiliating me than about harming the baby.

Slowly, my hands slide up his body until my arms are wrapped around his neck in a desperate embrace. He releases the tension of his hold on my neck, but the hand remains resting there, a reminder of what he'll do if I don't obey. Then, he assaults my mouth once more without giving me a chance to recover from what he's done.

He presses me into the wall, holding me there as he ravages my mouth, his tongue forcing its way inside again. I know I have no choice but to endure his sick desires as he uses me to satisfy himself. My tears flow freely although silent down my cheeks and I hope for an end at the feel of his arousal against me.

"Stop crying," he snarls after ending another long kiss. He wipes them away angrily and stares down at me, nostrils flaring before he finally steps away. "There, that wasn't so hard, was it?"

I rub my neck and give the only acceptable response. "No, Sir."

"Good. We will continue this in bed later, *ma souris.*"

My skin crawls at his words. I've been back for a while and now he wants to have sex with me, when I'm about to give birth any day?

"Don't think about it too hard," he says as he leads me to the door of his office with a strong grip on my arm. "You are never in control and it will be best if you don't try to fight me."

I know what he means and I try not to cry. There's no escaping my fate. He's determined to break me, body and soul.

"But first, you have an appointment with the doctor."

I'm surprised he's letting me see a doctor but I say nothing in response as he walks me toward one of the rooms near the front of the house.

Once we reach the door, he opens it for me. "I've had one of the rooms made into a room suitable for the delivery of our child. The doctor is here to examine you to determine when that will happen."

When the delivery will happen? I can't believe he's trying to control everything, including the baby's arrival into the world. What the hell is he up to?

I won't get any answers and as we walk inside, I spot the bed with the stirrups and involuntarily take a step back at the sight of the doctor standing by the bed. He doesn't blink as I enter the room and Gaspard leads the way over to the bed.

"Sit here." Gaspard guides me onto it and forces my feet into the stirrups. Since he only allows me to wear long skirts, there's nothing to remove and I turn my head away to look at anything except him as he lifts my skirt above my knees, baring me to the doctor while pulling off my underwear.

The doctor wastes no time coming closer. "This may be uncomfortable, girl, but I need to examine you. Please, try to relax."

Girl? Does he not look at me as if I'm a person either but merely Gaspard's property?

I close my eyes as I feel him between my legs, a lubed and gloved finger entering me. The precaution doesn't stop the hurt of his finger going inside and I can't help crying out, trying not to move as he moves his finger around and pushes in deeper.

"How close is she?" Gaspard asks. "She is far enough along to deliver, yes?"

"Any day now," the doctor says, his finger still inside me and making me squirm. "You wish to schedule the induction?"

I know what that means and despite my better judgment, words of protest escape anyway as I stare at the doctor. "What? No!"

"You will shut up," Gaspard snaps at me as the doctor removes his finger and slides the glove off. "It is time to have this child and I will not risk your health for some foolish idea of how things should happen naturally. You are my wife and this child is mine, it will be born according to my plan."

"Please..."

"Silence!" His voice thunders in the room and even the doctor flinches, but it is clear he's being paid to remain silent. He has kept his gaze on Gaspard and doesn't look at me although I stare at him hoping for him to recognize that this is all wrong.

I flinch, too, and go quiet, although it doesn't stop my eyes from tearing up at the idea of him forcing me to have the baby before I'm ready, all because he wants control. I close my eyes, refusing to look at either of them, and the conversation continues as if I'm not there. As if I don't matter.

"If the baby doesn't arrive by the end of the week, you will induce her on Sunday."

"Of course."

"And..." Gaspard chuckles, the sound grating on my ears, which heat at this question. "It will not harm the baby for me to try and... assist things along, correct?"

"No, not at all."

The two men laugh as I cringe. This doctor has to realize I'm not a willing participant and he isn't going to do anything. He thinks what Gaspard is doing is fine and laughing with him at the idea of using sex to try and induce natural labor before forcing it instead. What the fuck?

Gaspard helps me off the bed and I quickly adjust my dress, although the doctor has already seen me and Gaspard had his hands all over me anyway. He's disgusting, but it is clear the doctor is too, as he turns and heads toward the door, pausing to glance back at us.

"You know how to reach me," he says to Gaspard, "If the baby hasn't arrived by Sunday, I'll bring what we need for the procedure."

"Excellent." The doctor leaves and Gaspard grabs me by the upper arms, shaking me as his voice thunders. "How dare you speak to me that way in front of him! I told you to cease disrespecting me and it is clear you need a demonstration of what will happen if you do so again."

"Please," I beg him with tears in my eyes. "You'll hurt the baby. I'm just worried--"

"It is not your job to worry, *ma souris*. You are to listen to me, and do as I say, without question." Maintaining his grip on my arm, he drags me over to the opposite side of the room, and points at the couch. "Bend over the arm."

Oh god. He's going to hit me! My stomach clenches in fear and my palms grow sweaty. "I'm sorry," I whimper. "I'm really sorry."

"You will be," he sneers, beginning to undo his belt. "Now, do as you're told because every second you don't, the punishment will be worse."

I move toward the couch, feeling his eyes on me the whole time and knowing I'm not getting out of this. I've pushed him too far. I bend over the arm, doing my best to make sure I'm not putting pressure on my stomach, and slam my eyes shut at the clinking sound of his belt. I jump at the sound of the leather smacking against itself as he tests it and wait for the first hit.

"Lift your skirt and hold it, wife. You will accept your punishment on your bare ass to remind you of the consequences every time you sit."

Tears stream down my cheeks, but I don't dare cry out, afraid of what would happen if I do as I reach back and do as he's demanded.

"You will count," he snarls right before the first smack of the belt lands across my bare ass.

"One." I grit my teeth as I force the words out. I'm determined to stay strong through my terror and the inevitable pain.

Another smack and then he waits. "Count louder!"

"Two."

The word is strangled but his voice sounds satisfied as he says, "Do not forget this lesson," while bringing the belt down on my ass again.

"Three!" I scream the word through the pain and my resolve to stay quiet begins to crack as the hits keep coming, although he is careful not to hit anywhere that would risk the baby. He may be cruel, but he's not stupid enough to harm his child.

My tears flow freely when we reach ten and I'm barely able to speak. He doesn't stop.

"Eleven!" My voice cracks as I scream. "Please... I can't..."

He strikes me again and I'm sobbing. "Twelve! Please..." My ass is on fire and I fear I won't be able to sit if he continues. I fear that's what he wants in the end because he ignores my plea and the belt hits again. I try to get the words out through my tears. "Th-thirteen."

"You will not question me!"

Smack!

"F-fourteen!"

Smack!

I'ms sobbing so hard but manage to gasp out, "F...fif...fifteen."

The belt smacks into the floor and Gaspard grabs a fistful of my hair, yanking me up and off the couch. "What did you learn, *ma souris*?"

"N-not to..." I struggle to speak through the

sobs, his hold hurting me as he forces me to look him in the face. "Not to... question you."

"That's right. You are my wife and you will do as I say. Is that clear?"

"Yes, Sir." The words are choked out of my mouth as I repeat what he wants to hear. "I will not question you."

He releases me without further aggression and walks away, leaving me to stand there alone, trying to rub away the severe pain on my ass and crying until Eva comes in and helps me back to my room without a word spoken between us.

6

———

MADDIE

"Maddie?" Eva's worry filled voice reaches to me through a haze and I open my eyes, staring at the ceiling and feeling the dull pain of the welts on my ass.

"Yeah?" My voice comes out hoarse and Eva's face appears as she leans over me. "Are you alright? Did the lotion help?"

I don't want her to feel bad by telling her no, that my ass hurts as much as earlier when he hit me, when she tried so hard to help ease the pain. "Yes. I will... I will be okay."

"Maddie." Tears fill her eyes as she sits next to me on the bed. "You don't have to lie to me. I know it hurts."

"I just don't see the point in complaining."

"I know. I'm worried though."

She is sweet. Gaspard is definitely escalating

and ensuring his control. He showed me he isn't afraid to punish me for talking back or having any opinion or feeling outside of what he wants me to have. It's terrifying and I don't know what to do.

"I'm worried too." I sit up and put my arms around her, resting my chin on her shoulder as I close my eyes and we hold each other for a few moments.

"We need to do something, Maddie." Her voice is so soft and filled with tears, it breaks my heart.

"I'm afraid there's nothing we can do." I whisper back, unable to fathom how we can possibly escape this hell. "I know you said you've got a plan, but after tonight, I will be sleeping in his room. He is not going to let me out of his sight. And now... he's planning to have the baby born by the end of this week, Eva. I'm not sure how I'll be able to leave at all if that happens."

"Don't worry." She pulls back and cups my face. "We will figure it out, I promise."

I wish I could see that happening, but each day that passes, I fear escaping Gaspard again will never happen. I nod though, because I don't want her to know I'm close to giving up and doing my best to survive this situation because once my baby is born, all my focus will be on keeping her safe, even from her father.

She stands up. "You should get some rest."

With a shake of my head, I hold my hand out to her. "I can't. It's dinner time."

She helps me off the bed and I hiss at the pain.

"I wish you could take a bath." Eva sighs. "Maybe after dinner. It might help soothe the pain a little."

"Yeah, maybe."

That won't matter later, since he made it clear earlier that he expects to... enjoy my body later tonight.

I sigh as we walk slowly down to the dining room and try to hide my pain as we arrive. Gaspard is already seated and although I wince while sitting down in the chair next to him, as expected, he says nothing and smiles at me like he didn't hit me earlier.

"Wife." He waits until I meet his gaze and covers the hand I've rested on the table with his. "How are you feeling?"

"I'm... fine, thank you, Sir."

He smiles at me, his expression appreciating my canned response as he lifts my hand and kisses the back of it. "Good. After dinner, Eva will help you move into my room, *ma souris*. I will enjoy looking at your beautiful face every night."

His words make me sick and I want to run away from this man. Instead, I sit there in silence, letting him display his affection and wishing for this dinner to end while doing everything I can to hide my revulsion of him... and whatever comes next.

AFTER EVA HELPS ME BATHE, WE MOVE WHAT little belongings I have into Gaspard's room. She is quieter than usual and I ask her if she's alright.

"No, but that's life here," she says with a soft smile. "Will you be okay?"

We both know the answer to that question is no, but I nod as we finish putting my clothing away.

Gaspard enters the room then, with a drink in hand, and glares at Eva. "Get out."

She doesn't dare to look at me while leaving the room and Gaspard turns all his attention to me. I don't want to be here alone with him, but he's determined to make me suffer by making me his wife in every sense of the word.

I keep my eyes down and wait for him to say something. He walks toward me, and I take a step back, my heart pounding. He grasps my chin, lifting my head up to look at him, and I see the lust in his gaze.

"Sir..." I whisper. "I'm tired and--"

"Silence." The word isn't said harshly, but I know he wouldn't hesitate to make me if I don't stop begging him not to do this. He brings his lips to mine as he mutters, "You will share my bed tonight."

His tongue invades my mouth and I close my eyes, fighting the urge to vomit as he assaults my mouth. After several minutes of forcing himself on me, he ends the kiss and leads me over to the bed. He turns me so I'm facing away from him and there is a clink of the glass on the nightstand before his hands are on my bare legs. He slides my nightdress up and over my head, baring my naked body to his gaze before tossing it away. Then, he moves his hands to my hips, caressing them.

"You have been a bad wife," he says as he presses his body against my back and slides his hands around to cup my tender breasts. He pinches my nipples until I cry out and he nips my ear. "Do you deny it?"

As if I would dare. "N-no, Sir." My voice trembles at his touch as he continues to pinch and tug on my nipples, making me feel sick.

"That's right, you can't." He tugs harder and I gasp, my knees nearly buckling as he whispers, "Bad wives must be punished."

I sob from the pain as his hands grab my ass, squeezing and reminding me of the abuse he caused earlier. I know better than to try and move away and stay still as he squeezes my ass cheeks harder and then slaps my ass.

"Turn around and lay on your back, *ma souris*."

He releases me and I turn to face him before sitting on the edge of the bed and leaning until my back touches the duvet covered mattress. "Now, spread your legs wide and place your hands over your head."

I do as he's told me, despite the fact I know it means he will see all of me, and my body trembles as he sits next to me and places his hand on my belly.

"This is my child," he says as he glides his hand down, rubbing between my legs. "And this... is mine, forever."

I hate him. I would spit at him if it wouldn't result in a worse punishment than earlier. I want to vomit as he strokes me, forcing my body to respond to his touch and I close my eyes so I don't have to look at him while he does it.

"Don't hide from me," he snaps and I open my eyes as his hand stills between my legs. "Your body is mine, wife. I will touch you, and you will allow it. Do not forget this lesson again."

My face burns as I whisper, "I won't."

"Good. Now, I will fuck you." His fingers stroke me again, spreading my wetness and making it harder to ignore my body's response, hatred burning in my chest the longer he does it. Then, he stands and I force myself to watch as he undresses, my stomach churning at the sight of his arousal as he stands there fully naked.

"Please," I beg him. "I don't feel well."

"Silence!" He slams his hands down on the bed, on either side of my head, and hovers over me as he glares. "You have no say in what happens. You will take me into your body and be a good wife. Understood?"

"Yes, Sir."

He repositions himself at the end of the bed and says, "Wrap your legs around me."

I obey him, trying to breathe through the panic I feel as he shifts his body, rubbing himself against me and then he smiles, taunting me. "You are wet for me, wife."

"No..."

He laughs, once more placing his hand between my legs and forcing me to listen to the sound of my wetness. To him, proof of my arousal, even though I know my body is responding to the touch, preparing itself for the inevitable assault.

I want to cry and scream, but I can do nothing except lay there frozen as he once again takes something from me he has no right to, and before the night is out, the burning desire to make him pay for what he's done to me.

It feels like hours pass as he uses me, my body bruised and sore at the end, while he's got a satisfied smile on his lips.

"Good wife," he says as he climbs off me, taking me in as I lay there, unable to move and fighting back tears as he rolls over and leaves the bed. "Go to sleep now."

I was hoping he would settle in beside me and fall asleep so I could go wash off his disgusting and vile touch, but he winks at me and after making sure I'm beneath the covers, pulls something from beside the bed.

My eyes widen at the sight of a cuff linked to a chain. It's thick and he locks it around my ankle, clicking it and testing to make sure it's secure but not too tight.

"I cannot trust you, wife, and this is to ensure you do not leave my room until I release you in the morning."

I'm too tired and sore to fight him as he kisses my forehead, then puts on a robe that's hanging on the back of the door, before turning off the light and leaving me alone in the dark room.

A sob escapes at the thought of being a prisoner in his bed, too. I want to run away, but I've learned my lesson. It isn't going to happen at this point. I need to bide my time and be patient, no matter how painful that might be.

THE NEXT MORNING, I WAKE UP AND THE previous night is right there, assaulting my senses with the pain of my ass and the stickiness between my thighs. Gaspard forced himself on me and succeeded in making me feel like nothing, especially when he placed a restraint around my ankle like I'm fucking animal.

How humiliating and degrading. If he wanted to make sure I understand how vulnerable I am, he's succeeded. And what if I had needed to use the restroom in the middle of the night?

I have no doubt he probably would've let me piss myself rather than release the cuff to allow me that simple kindness.

Gaspard rolls over then and throws his arm around me, pulling me toward him as much as possible with my stomach between us. I don't fight and after a few moments, he opens his eyes and smiles at me.

"Good morning, wife." His voice is husky and he runs a hand down my arm, his gaze soft while looking at me for what is probably the first time ever. "Did you sleep well?"

"Yes, Sir." I murmur, lowering my gaze until he tilts my chin with one finger and forces me to look at him.

I whimper as he kisses my lips, opening up for him as he expects because I honestly have no fight in me this morning. And he must realize that because he says, "You were a good wife last night, *ma souris.*"

I think today will be a good day until he continues with, "You will stay here today and show me what you have learned about obedience. I will have Eva bring you meals today, but you are not to leave this room, hm?"

Nodding, he reaches down and releases the ankle cuff. "Relieve yourself and bathe. I will see you tonight."

Saying nothing, I slip from the bed and head toward the in-suite bathroom.

"Oh, and *ma souris.* One final thing..." He opens the bedroom door as I turn toward him, only to stare in horror at the sight of Eva entering the room with a tray of food, her mouth covered so that she can't speak.

Gaspard's usual cruel expression returns as he takes the tray of food and says, "Eva and you will no longer spend time together. Her job is to ensure you eat when you are confined to this room and nothing else. As you can see, she is gagged, and a guard will make sure she remains that way when in contact with you."

Eva stares at me, eyes wide and tears sliding

down her cheek, until Gaspard says, "That will be all Eva. You will return with her tray at lunch and leave it outside the door."

If this were anyone except Gaspard, I would ask why he would even bother allowing her any contact with me at all, but this is what he does. He will torture us both by reminding us of what we had... and what he took away from us.

She leaves and so does he after placing the tray on the table in the corner of the room, leaving me alone in the room, standing there naked, and feeling like shit. He will do anything to prevent me leaving again, including taking away the one person I feel safe with in this hellhole. I close my eyes, struggling to breathe and fighting the urge to cry.

The baby kicks, distracting me from my thoughts, and I rest my hand on my stomach. She's restless, probably picking up on my emotions.

"It will be okay," I tell her, even as my heart is breaking.

But it won't be okay, and after using the bathroom, I force down my breakfast while barely tasting it, wondering what I am going to do all day because the one thing I don't care to do is anger Gaspard by daring to leave this room.

7

MADDIE

Being stuck in the room all day makes the day drag.

After bathing and eating breakfast, I put the tray outside the room and close the door. There is too much temptation to step outside otherwise and I don't want any accusations of having so much as crossed the threshold with a single toe getting back to Gaspard.

Walking around the room, I try to find something to do and to my surprise, discover a hidden TV. Picking up the remote laying beside it, I turn it on, only to discover there aren't many available channels as many of them are blocked, requiring a passcode. There is one, though, and although the show is in black and white, I laugh at the silly antics of the main characters, reminding me of a happier time when my mother was alive and before my father died.

They loved each other so much. Even when times were tough, they had each other and laughed at the silliest things. We spent so much time doing fun things like going to zoo and my father reading me stories at bedtime. Every night he would tell me how much he loved me, kiss me goodnight, and tell me now it was time for him to dance with my mother in the kitchen. I don't know if they did, since I was younger and he always said that when I was going to bed, but my parent's love seemed magical.

I miss them so much, I cry every time I think about them.

My chest heaves as I try to catch my breath, fingers digging into my palms as I squeeze them together. The room is silent now, the laughter and chatter of the show long since replaced by the oppressive quiet of the empty house. I can hear the ticking of the clock on the wall, each second stretching into an eternity as I sit there, staring blankly ahead.

I hate being here. I hate the way Gaspard looks at me, the way his eyes roam over my body as if I'm nothing more than a piece of meat. I hate the way he talks to me, the way he treats me as if I'm less than human. I hate the way he touches me, the way his hands leave bruises on my skin that linger for days.

This isn't the life I envisioned for myself. This isn't a proper marriage; one where I am loved and cherished and a true partner to the man who loves me. Instead, I'm trapped in a hellish existence, bound to a man who sees me only as a means to an end. A man who doesn't care about me, who doesn't love me, who only wants one thing from me: a child. And a male one at that, which he isn't getting now, and fully plans on achieving at some point.

I wish something terrible would happen to Gaspard. I wish he would suffer, the way I suffer every day. I wish he would feel the pain I feel, the despair that consumes me as I sit here, weeping into my hands. I wish he could understand what it's like to be trapped in a marriage like this, to be treated like a piece of meat instead of a person.

But I know that wishing won't change anything. I know that Gaspard is powerful, that he has connections and resources I could never hope to match. I know that he will do whatever it takes to keep me here, to keep his hands on me, to keep me pregnant against my will. I know that I am trapped and that there probably is no escape.

And so, I weep. Crying for the life I could have had, for the love I could have found, and for the freedom I could have known. Also, I cry for the child growing inside me, who will be born into this hellish existence and raised by a man who doesn't love her and will never love her because he isn't capable of loving anyone. There's no good here, nothing except pain and suffering.

After all, to him, I'm not a person, but rather an object. He never uses my name when speaking to me; instead, he refers to me as "mouse" or "wife," and sometimes, when he's angry, other names such as 'bitch.' He has dehumanized me and each day, it becomes harder to not give up completely in an attempt to survive the indescribable pain of this lonely and isolated existence.

"It's not fair." The words exit my mouth in a whisper as I wipe angrily at the tears sliding down my cheeks. "I wish he would fucking die..."

I jump at the unexpected sound of Gaspard's laughter, my gaze jerking up from where it stares blindly at the television to see him standing in the doorway, holding my lunch tray. He smiles and says, "Is that any way for a wife to speak about her husband?"

"N-no." I stumble over the words. "Sir, I didn't think you'd be back until later."

He enters the room and I can do nothing except watch as he places the tray down and walks toward me. I don't dare look away.

"Well, it is a good thing I came by, hm? You seem to be missing a few... things."

I have no idea what he means and my heart beats faster in my chest. Is he going to punish me for what I said? Or because I cried?

He sits beside me on the bed and although I'm afraid, I say nothing as he takes my hand and lifts it to his mouth, kissing the back of it. I want to rip my hand out of his, but I don't, and lower my gaze to hide my revulsion.

"What is wrong, *ma souris?*" His voice is softer than normal, although I still hear the taunt behind it as he continues. "Is there something you wish to share with me?"

"No, Sir."

His eyes narrow, but he says nothing more as he stands. "Eat your lunch, wife, and in a little while, we will take a walk. Some fresh air will be good for us, hm?"

A walk? Is this a trick after he told me to stay in the room all day? I don't dare question him, though, and maybe that's why he said that, to test me and see if I'm learning the lesson he beat into me yesterday. So all I do is nod in response and respond with a meek, "Yes, Sir."

He leaves me alone and I glance towards the tray as the door closes behind him. I have no appetite, but know better than to risk him finding me untouched food. Sighing, I stand up and walk over to eat the sandwich and soup.

After finishing, I make sure to place the tray outside before heading to the bathroom to relieve myself and freshen up.

I yawn while waiting for him, so I lie down to rest before our walk since that's bound to tire me out all over again once we're done. I fall asleep within minutes and sleep fitfully until I am suddenly awakened by the sensation of someone touching my breasts.

I jolt awake, my heart pounding in my chest as I take in the sight of Gaspard on the bed beside me. He's lowered the straps of my nightgown, exposing my breasts, and as I struggle to sit up in my groggy state, he seizes me and presses me back down, forcing one of my nipples into his mouth and sucking on it until it's agonizingly rigid.

I want to beg him to stop, yet the words catch in my throat. I'm frozen, more fearful of another punishment than anything else. When he switches to the other nipple, he biting down on it until I cry out. Even then, I let my sobs speak for me.

"You are learning, wife." He licks each nipple, soothing the pain a little with his wet tongue, before sliding a hand down the center of my body and over my stomach before sliding down between my legs. "A little pain can bring a lot of pleasure, *ma souris*. What do you think, hm? Are you wet for me?"

I recoil at his touch, filled with disgust for the way he forces me to submit to his cruel hands. My instinct is to clamp my legs shut, to deny him any access to my body. But I know better now. I understand that my body's response—the warmth and wetness—is a natural reaction, not a sign of enjoyment. And so I endure, gritting my teeth against the humiliation and the pain.

"See?" His fingers stroke me, forcing my body to respond further, and his laughter is taunting. "You enjoy this, *ma souris*. There is no need to be ashamed. You are turned on by your husband's touch, as you should be."

I grit my teeth, my face heating. I force myself to say nothing, such as shouting and curse at him, to avoid him hurting me, especially as he forces two fingers inside me while using his thumb to rub against my clit. My body betrays me as it responds rapidly to his expert touch, the orgasm swift and unwanted.

Gaspard chuckles and says, "watch" while lifting his fingers to his mouth and licking them clean. "Delicious. Now, it is time for you to pleasure me."

My heart races as I realize what he wants from me. I've never done this before, and the thought of submitting to his cruel hands fills me with dread.

Gaspard looms over me, his eyes gleaming with anticipation. "Come on, *ma souris*. Don't be shy. Show me what you can do."

I draw a deep breath and gather the strength to face what lies ahead. As my fingers make contact with his skin, a sense of helplessness envelops me. I begin to explore his form, attempting to push aside the nausea and terror that threaten to consume me. Rather than succumbing to emotions, I concentrate on doing what he wants, pleasing him in order to avoid any additional torment.

Gaspard watches me with a predatory smile, enjoying the sight of me submitting to his will. "That's it, *ma souris*. You've done well. Now lay back and spread those legs for me, *salope*."

He starts to strip while stepping in between my legs after I've moved into an acceptable position, but as he takes off his shirt, I cry out in pain. Grabbing my stomach, I roll to the side, moaning as my abdomen contracts and there's a sudden rush of wetness between my legs.

Gaspard's voice is practically gleeful as he exclaims, "Your water has broken, wife."

Gaspard doesn't try to comfort me as I lie there with my eyes clenched shut, crying out as a contraction hits and fear floods my system. I'm not ready!

"Guard!" The door creaks and Gaspard barks at order at whoever walked into the room. "She's in labor. Pick her up and carry her to the room I prepared downstairs."

There's no verbal response, only a strong pair of arms lifting me from the bed and supporting me completely as they carry me down the hallway. Another contraction hits as we enter the room he wants me in and I scream, "Something's wrong! It ... hurts so bad."

As the guard places me on the prepared hospital bed, Gaspard snaps at me, "There's nothing wrong." With that, he talks out his phone and dials, barking in it, "Her water has broken. Get here quickly."

I cling to the sheets, my knuckles white as the contractions continue to wrack my body. Time seems to slow to a crawl as I wait for the doctor, my mind foggy with pain and fear.

Gaspard's voice cuts through the haze, reciting the details of my labor to the doctor upon his arrival. I can't even muster the strength to open my eyes, every ounce of my being focused on riding out the waves of agony that threaten to consume me.

The doctor's touch is cool and sterile as he finally examines me, and I flinch with each probing finger. When he finally declares that I am fully dilated and ready to push, I can barely believe it. The thought of pushing a baby out is both terrifying and exhilarating, a mix of emotions that leaves me breathless.

I grit my teeth and bear down, my body responding instinctively to the doctor's instructions. Each push sends a new wave of pain coursing through me, yet with each contraction, I feel a growing sense of determination. I won't let the pain defeat me; I'm stronger than that.

As the minutes tick by, I can sense the room growing tense. I push each time the doctor says to, my body straining with each effort. And then, finally, I feel a sudden, searing pain that is followed by a rush of relief as my daughter arrives into the cruel world I share with her monster of a father.

Her tiny, wailing cry fills me with a love and joy I never knew existed. Even though the pain is still there, intense and all-consuming, hearing my daughter alive and well is worth it.

And that's the last thought I have before passing out after the doctor places a mask over my face.

8

MADDIE

A BABY CRIES.

Everything is hazy and someone touches my hand. I open my eyes... don't I?

A woman's voice speaks, but it isn't Eva. "You must feed the child."

I feel something against my bare chest, and suddenly register that it's my sweet baby girl. Her tiny hands grip my skin, searching, and her mouth finally connects with my nipple. The sensation is strange and uncomfortable, like nothing I've ever experienced before. It hurts, but I don't pull away. I recognize she needs to eat, holding her securely with both hands, even though my eyes won't open for some reason.

The world around me is hazy, but I can feel her weight, her warmth, and the rhythmic pull of her suckling. It's a strange and surreal experience, and I focus on the way she smells to remain calm.

A door opens and Gaspard's voice reaches me from across the room, "Is there a problem?"

The woman's reply is terse. "No. The child was hungry."

"And my wife?"

Whoever this lady is, she clucks her tongue. "She responds to commands. Otherwise, she is unaware."

"Good." He lowers his voice as he asks her, "You understand my instructions?"

"Yes. She will feed the child until her supply is steady and then pump to limit..."

The woman's voice fades away. The warmth of my baby's small form and the rhythmic pull of her suckling are the only things keeping me grounded in this surreal situation. My desire to sleep grows and I can feel my energy draining as the baby continues to feed. I fight to stay awake but the exhaustion proves too much. As the baby detaches from my breast, and she's gone from my chest, I slip into a deep, dreamless sleep.

"WHAT...?"

I blink at the light shining through the blinds,

lifting my hand to block it out only for the motion to take longer than it should and I drop my useless hand to the bed. Why do I feel so drowsy and heavy?

"Ah, *ma souris*. You are awake." Why can't I see him? I try to lift my head off the pillow, but it feels like too much as well, and I flinch when Gaspard leans into view, his grin bordering on menacing. "It is the medicine, wife. Don't worry, it will wear off in a few hours."

I don't understand. My lips are dry and as I open my mouth to speak, the dryness of my throat has me coughing instead. "Um..." I manage to croak out. "Water...?"

He nods, leaving my view for a moment before returning with a glass and a straw. He lifts my head carefully, bringing the straw to my mouth, and I take several sips, before he lowers me back down onto the pillow.

"Wh-what... happened?" I try to recall the memories, but the last thing I remember is giving birth. "The baby... where is she?"

"Do not worry. Emilie is with the nurse."

My lip wobbles. His word means nothing to me; my need to see my daughter outweighs the lesson I learned about questioning him. "Please, let me see her."

"No. You are to rest."

Tears slip down my cheeks, yet I can't even lift my hands to wipe them away.

There's a cruel twist to his lips as he stares at me before saying, "It does no good to cry, *ma souris*. Sleep now."

It appears I really have no choice because a sudden wave of tiredness rushes over me and the last thing I hear is Gaspard whispering, "Sweet dreams, wife."

WAKING UP IN GASPARD'S BED IS disorienting. I have no idea what day it is or how long it's been since I gave birth, although I no longer feel weighed down.

He's sleeping beside me when I wake up and after noticing my leg isn't cuffed, I slip out of the bed and start to walk slowly toward the bathroom, but... where is the pain between my legs? I feel none, which is strange after giving birth. Maybe the doctor gave me something to help?

Too tired to care enough to question it, I turn on the water in the shower because I feel gross. i slip out of the nightgown I'm wearing and step into shower, sighing in relief as the hot water runs over my body.

After a minute, I'm fully awake, and wash quickly, grooming myself as well before turning off the water and stepping out as my brain finally blares at me.

Where the hell is my baby?

I wrap the towel around me and walk out into the bedroom, going to the closet to pull out a dress, and that's when I see myself in the full-length mirror. My belly is only a little curved, while my breasts are full and ache, the nipples a bit more red than I've ever seen them before. But it's my stomach... is that normal? Does it just go down like that immediately?

I'm not sure. I never thought about it before, but I would think it would take longer for it to look normal again.

There's a noise behind me, but I'm so lost in thought it barely registers until Gaspard is right behind me, naked and his erection pressing against my back as he meets my gaze in the mirror. He reaches up, his fingers sliding around my neck, squeezing a little as he says, "It is good to see you awake, *ma souris.*"

I whimper, freezing in his hold, and meet his gaze in the mirror as I softly ask, "Where is she, Sir? I want to see her."

"Hmm." He slides his hands down my body and

cups both breasts in his hands, squeezing enough to make it hurt a bit. "She's with the nurse. You will see her after breakfast."

What? I need to see her now. It's been so long... how long?

"Sir... how long has it been?"

"Since the birth?"

"Yes."

He shrugs. "Almost four weeks, but the nurse will discuss the details with you. I know nothing of these things."

"Four weeks?" Tears well up in my eyes and I forget everything except my desperation to see my baby even though I don't understand why it has been that long. "Please, Sir..."

"Question me again and there will be consequences, wife." He turns me around and I stare at his chest, unwilling to look at him and knowing he hates that. His hands grip my arms tightly as he says, "You will do as you're told. Now, dress for breakfast and after you will meet the nurse."

I can only nod and as I pull the dress on, he leaves me alone.

Sitting in front of the mirror, I brush my hair, tears silently falling down my cheeks. I want to see my daughter; I want to know what is happening and why Gaspard has kept me drugged while keeping me away from our baby.

"It is time." Gaspard appears in the mirror, dressed now, and as our eyes meet, I wipe my tears away and stand up. He frowns at the sight of my tears, but he says nothing as he offers his arm. "Let us have breakfast."

"Yes, Sir." I whisper, placing my hand on his arm.

He leads me to the dining room and sits next to me instead of across the table. An older woman I don't recognize enters the room, her eyes widening slightly when she sees me, but she says nothing while serving the food. It's nothing fancy, only simple eggs, yogurt, some fruit and toast, but it tastes so good.

Breakfast feels like it takes forever, and when I'm finished eating, I wait quietly for Gaspard to finish.

He smiles as he wipes his mouth, standing up. "Go with the nurse and she will answer your questions, *ma souris*."

"Thank you, Sir." I whisper as I stand up. "What about Emilie?"

"Later." His eyes narrow. "Now go."

～

THE NURSE LEADS ME DOWN A LONG HALLWAY, and I can't help but feel like I'm being led to my execution. My heart races as we approach a door, and she opens it, revealing a small nursery with a crib in the corner.

My baby girl is inside, sleeping peacefully, her tiny fingers curled around her blanket. I gasp, my heart swelling with love as I rush to her side. The nurse watches me closely, and I can't help but feel like she's judging me.

"She's beautiful," I whisper, reaching out to touch her soft cheek. "How is she?"

The nurse clears her throat. "She is healthy. You were given a drug to ease pain while making sure you could follow commands and eat while allowing your milk to come in and then to pump. The baby is now strictly bottle-fed with your milk."

"What?" My heart aches at the thought of Gaspard separating me from my daughter in every way. "Why can't I breastfeed her? I remember doing that before..."

The nurse looks at me sympathetically. "I'm sorry, Madame. I don't know the reasons behind it. But you're here now, and you can spend some time with your baby."

Of course. She's hired by Gaspard; she's not going to answer my questions or tell me why as she likely doesn't know. Simply following orders like everyone else.

I nod, my eyes never leaving my daughter's face even as silent tears slide down my cheeks. "Thank you."

She hands me a lukewarm bottle and says, "It's time to feed her," before leaving the room and shutting the door behind her.

Picking up Emilie, she opens her eyes and coos. Her mouth open and closes as she searches for food and because I want to enjoy the short time I have with her today, I have a huge desire to unbutton my dress and allow her to feed from my breasts as she should. I don't, though, as the nurse will probably be required to report to Gaspard about that if she sees I didn't use the bottle.

Instead, I sit in the rocking chair in the corner of the room, and watch my daughter suck the nipple of the bottle. One hand holds the bottle and the other... well, she's wrapped her little fingers around my index finger and we gaze into each other's eyes.

The urge to cry is strong as the ticking of the clock on the wall alerts me to the minutes passing by, my little girl soon finishing her bottle after I gently burp her twice, and before I can blink, the nurse has returned to the room.

"I'm sorry, Madame. You must leave now."

A tear slides down my cheek as she gently takes Emilie from my arms and walks her over to the crib.

"Do you take care of her?"

"Yes, Madame," she replies without looking at me. "During the day. There is a night nurse as well. The baby is never alone."

She should be with me, I want to scream. It isn't her fault though, it is Gaspard's and his cruel need to control, as always.

The nurse turns to me and softly pleads, "Please, Madame. Go. I don't wish for you to get in trouble and the child is safe with me."

My heart aches with every beat. Tears continue to leak from my eyes at having to leave my baby with the nurse, another woman who cares for her instead of me. With nothing I can say or do to change this, I steal one long final glance at my daughter for the evening and leave the room, sobbing quietly all the way back to the bedroom.

The weight of Gaspard's cruelty bears down on me as I collapse onto the bed, my body shaking with grief. I curl into a ball and wrap my arms around my knees, trying to find some semblance of comfort in the darkness. But it's no use. The reality of my situation is too overwhelming, and almost too painful to bear any longer.

And as I cry myself to sleep, it is impossible for me not to wonder... what kind of future will Emilie have? Will she grow up knowing the love and care of a loving mother, or will she be just another pawn in Gaspard's twisted game of power and control? The thought is excruciating, and as I drift into a fitful sleep, I'm haunted by the fears and uncertainties of what is yet to come.

9

———

MADDIE

THE MORNING LIGHT FILTERS THROUGH THE heavy curtains as I sit at the vanity, staring at my reflection while Eva brushes my hair. My face looks pale, hollow in places it shouldn't be, and there are dark circles under my eyes that no amount of concealer seems to hide.

Eva's movements are gentle as she works, but I can see the concern in her eyes reflected in the mirror. The gag in her mouth prevents her from speaking, but her worried expression tells me everything she would say if she could.

I know she thinks I need to eat more, need to take better care of myself, but eating has become difficult when every meal feels like another step deeper into this nightmare.

Catching her gaze in the mirror, I give the slightest nod, acknowledging her unspoken worry.

Her eyes grow sad, and she places a brief, comforting hand on my shoulder.

The door opens without a knock, it never does anymore, and Gaspard strides in wearing one of his expensive suits. His eyes rake over me with that familiar possessive gleam.

"Good morning, *ma souris*." He approaches and places his hands on my shoulders, squeezing just hard enough to remind me of his strength. "Today is an important day. We have much to discuss."

Eva immediately steps back, her eyes downcast as she sets the brush on the vanity.

"Wait outside the door," Gaspard commands, and Eva hurries from the room without a word, her gagged silence making her departure even more haunting.

I remain seated, my hands folded in my lap, waiting. He loves these moments when he has my complete attention, when he can reveal whatever new torture he's devised.

"I have wonderful news, *ma souris*." His reflection grins at me in the mirror. "You will be joining me at campaign events now. The public is eager to see my beautiful wife supporting her husband."

My stomach drops. Public appearances mean exposure, cameras, people watching. It means pretending to be happy while standing next to the man who has destroyed my life.

"I..." I start, then stop myself. Expressing concern will only anger him.

"You what?" His hands tighten on my shoulders.

"I'm honored to support you, Sir." The words taste like poison on my tongue.

"Good girl." He leans down to kiss the top of my head, and I force myself not to flinch. "We'll start small—a few local events. But eventually, you'll be by my side at every major appearance. My devoted wife, showing the world what a strong marriage looks like."

The irony would be laughable if it weren't so horrifying.

"Of course, Sir. Whatever you need."

He straightens, smoothing his tie in the mirror. "I know this is new for you, but you'll adjust. You always do." His smile is cold. "And remember, every moment we're in public, every word you speak, every expression on your face? It all reflects on me. I trust you understand the importance of that."

The threat is clear. Behave, or face the consequences later.

"I understand completely."

"Excellent. Eva will help you choose

appropriate clothing for today's event. Something that shows you're a woman of substance, but not too... attention-grabbing." His eyes linger on my reflection. "We wouldn't want to give the wrong impression."

After he leaves, I remain at the vanity, staring at myself. This is my life now; performing for crowds, pretending to love a man who sees me as property. But as I sit here, something shifts inside me.

If I have to be in public, around people, maybe there's an opportunity I haven't considered. Maybe being visible isn't just another prison; maybe it's a chance.

The thought is dangerous, but it gives me something I haven't had in months: hope.

Later, Eva returns to help me dress, and I catch her eye in the mirror.

"Eva," I whisper, "do you think... do you think things can change?"

She pauses in her work, her hands stilling on the zipper of my dress. After a moment, she gives the slightest nod, and I know we're both thinking the same thing.

Someday, somehow, I need to find a way out of this. Not just for me, but for Emilie. She deserves better than growing up in a house ruled by a monster.

And perhaps these public appearances will give me the chance I've been waiting for.

THE CROWD STRETCHES BEFORE US, HUNDREDS of faces looking up expectantly at the platform where Gaspard and I stand. My heart pounds so hard I'm sure everyone can hear it, but I keep my expression serene, my smile fixed in place.

Gaspard's hand rests on the small of my back, a gesture that might look supportive to the crowd but feels like a brand marking his ownership.

"My friends," he begins, his voice carrying easily over the microphone, "I stand before you today not just as your mayor, but as a man who has overcome tremendous personal challenges to find extraordinary happiness."

My stomach churns, but I maintain my smile.

"Many of you followed the story when my beloved stepdaughter went missing. Those were the darkest days of my life." His voice catches with perfectly manufactured emotion. "What I couldn't tell you then, what I was too ashamed to admit, was that Madeline didn't disappear because of some stranger. She left because she was struggling with feelings she thought were wrong."

The crowd murmurs, leaning in closer.

"You see, as Madeline grew into a beautiful young woman, we both began to feel something deeper than a typical stepfather-daughter relationship. She was horrified by these feelings, thought they made her a terrible person. So she ran, convinced she was betraying her mother's memory by falling in love with me."

Lie. All of it, lies. But I can see some faces in the crowd softening with understanding.

"I searched for months, not just because I was worried about her safety, but because I knew that what we felt was real. That love, true love, doesn't follow society's conventional rules." His hand presses harder against my back. "When she finally came home, we both realized we couldn't fight what was meant to be."

This is my cue. I step closer to the microphone, my voice somehow steady despite the screaming in my head.

"I was so confused, so afraid of what people would think." The words came out smoothly despite my disgust and fear. "But Gaspard helped me understand that love isn't something to be ashamed of. He waited for me, never gave up on us, and showed me that what we have is beautiful, not wrong."

The crowd applauds, and I see faces that look

genuinely moved by our "love story." If only they knew the truth.

"Madeline chose to come home to me," Gaspard continues, his arm sliding around my waist. "She chose love over fear, chose our future together. And now, as my wife, she stands beside me not just as my partner in life, but as my partner in serving this great city."

When he mentions "the family we're building together" and places his hand on my stomach, I have to bite the inside of my cheek to keep from crying out. The implication is clear: he wants people to think I'm pregnant.

Finally, mercifully, the speech ends. Gaspard waves to the crowd, his arm around my waist as cameras flash. I wave too, playing my part perfectly.

As we descend from the platform, his grip on my hand tightens painfully.

"Perfect performance, *ma souris*," he murmurs in my ear. "They're completely convinced. Though you looked a bit pale toward the end. We'll work on that for next time."

I want to throw up.

Next time. There will be too many next times.

And as we approach the car, there is Antosha, staring at me from where he's partially hidden. My lips part from the instinctual urge to call out, but

I'm afraid to breathe a word, to have Gaspard follow my gaze and see that he's here.

Gaspard guides me into the car, ending my connection with the man I actually love and I want to sob from knowing he's so close and yet impossible to get to.

The drive home passes in silence. I stare out the window, watching the world go by, thinking about all the people living their normal lives while I'm trapped in this nightmare. Of how Antosha just had to watch me lie and declare to the city how much I love Gaspard.

Back at the house, I try to head straight for my room, desperate for a few minutes alone to collect myself. But Gaspard stops me in the hallway.

"Where are you going? It's almost time for dinner."

"I thought I might rest for a moment—"

"Nonsense. You can rest after you eat." He checks his watch. "I have calls to make about the campaign. You'll dine alone tonight."

My heart sinks. Dining alone means no visit with Emilie afterward. Those precious minutes with my daughter are the only thing keeping me sane.

"But what about—"

He cuts me off. "What about what, *ma souris?*" His voice carries a warning.

"Nothing, Sir." I swallow my fear, holding back the tears that beg to flow. "I'll go to the dining room now."

He nods, already turning away, dismissing me.

I eat mechanically, tasting nothing, my thoughts on the little girl I won't get to hold tonight. When I finally make it to my room, I collapse on the bed and allow myself to cry for the first time in weeks.

The tears come quietly, years of training having taught me to grieve in silence. I cry for Emilie, sleeping alone in her nursery. I cry for the life I'll never have, for the freedom that seems more impossible with each passing day.

But mostly, I cry because I'm starting to lose hope that anyone will ever come for me, especially with the horrible lies Gaspard makes me support.

And without hope, I don't know how much longer I can survive this.

10

ANTOSHA

The annulment papers feel heavy in my hands as I stand in my uncle's study, the official seal still fresh on the documents. Six months of legal proceedings, finally over.

"It's done then," Guillame says from behind his desk, his tone carefully neutral but his disapproval evident in the tight line of his mouth.

"Yes." I set the papers down, my hands trembling slightly—whether from relief or anticipation, I can't say. "Léonie and I are both free now."

"Free." He repeats the word like it tastes bitter. "And what do you intend to do with this freedom, nephew?"

I meet his gaze directly, knowing he won't like my answer. "I'm going to get Madeline back."

Guillame closes his eyes and pinches the bridge

of his nose, a gesture I've seen countless times when he's trying to control his temper. "Antosha, we've discussed this. Malveaux is—"

"I don't care how powerful he is." The words come out harsher than I intended, months of frustration and helplessness boiling over. "She's been in that hell for eight months, Uncle. Eight months while I sat here doing nothing, playing the dutiful husband to a woman who never wanted me any more than I wanted her."

"You weren't doing nothing. You were protecting yourself, protecting this family—"

"Protecting myself?" I laugh, the sound bitter. "While Madeline suffers God knows what at his hands? While her daughter grows up in that house with that monster?"

Guillame's expression softens slightly. "You think I don't care what happens to her? That girl lived in this house, ate at our table. I would have married her myself to keep her safe. But rushing in blindly will only get you killed, and it won't help her."

I begin pacing, unable to stand still when every fiber of my being is screaming to act. "Then what do you suggest? That we continue to sit here while he destroys what's left of her spirit? I've seen the news footage, Uncle. She looks like a ghost of herself."

"I suggest we be smart about this." He stands and moves to the window, gazing out at the grounds. "If we're going to do this—and I'm not saying we should—we need information. We need allies. We need a plan that doesn't end with all of us dead and Madeline worse off than before."

Hope flickers in my chest for the first time in months. "You'll help me?"

He turns back to face me, his expression grave. "Against my better judgment, yes. That girl trusted us to protect her, and we failed. I won't fail her again." He holds up a warning finger. "But we do this my way. Carefully. Methodically. One mistake and we lose everything."

"Agreed." I feel like I can breathe properly for the first time since she was taken. "When do we start?"

"Tomorrow. I have some contacts who might be willing to help, people who owe me favors." He moves back to his desk, already shifting into planning mode. "But Antosha, you need to understand—this won't be quick. It could take months, maybe longer."

"I don't care how long it takes." I think of her face on that TV screen, the hollow emptiness in her eyes. "She's waited this long. I won't abandon her."

Guillame nods slowly. "Then we begin

tomorrow. But promise me something—you'll be careful. I've already lost too much family. I won't lose you too."

"I promise." The words feel like a vow. "I'm going to bring her home, Uncle. Whatever it costs."

As he dismisses me and I head toward the door, his voice stops me.

"Antosha? That girl... she meant something to you, didn't she? More than just duty or protection?"

I pause, my hand on the doorknob. There's no point in hiding it anymore. "Yes. She means everything."

"Then God help us both," he murmurs. "Because men in love do foolish things."

I don't argue with him. He's right—love makes men reckless, desperate, willing to risk everything for a chance at salvation. But as I close the door behind me, I know that same love is the only thing that's kept me sane these past months.

And it's the only thing that will give me the strength to face whatever comes next.

THE CAMPAIGN RALLY BUZZES WITH ENERGY AS I push through the crowd, my baseball cap pulled low and sunglasses hiding my identity. I shouldn't be here—it's reckless, dangerous—but I had to see her with my own eyes.

When Gaspard takes the podium, the crowd quiets, but my attention is entirely focused on the figure beside him. My heart nearly stops.

Madeline stands there in a pale blue dress, her smile perfectly composed, but I can see what others can't—the way her shoulders are held too rigidly, the slight tremor in her hands before she clasps them together. She's lost weight, her cheekbones more prominent than they should be, and there are shadows under her eyes that makeup can't quite hide.

But it's her expression that destroys me. The vibrant, spirited girl I fell in love with has been replaced by someone going through the motions of living. Her smile never reaches her eyes, and when she looks out at the crowd, it's like she's seeing through them, not at them.

Gaspard begins his speech, spinning his lies about their "unconventional love story," and I watch Madeline's face carefully. A muscle in her jaw ticks almost imperceptibly when he talks about her "choosing" to come back to him. Her fingers tighten around each other the more he speaks.

She's performing, playing a role, and it's killing her.

When she steps forward to speak, her voice is

steady but hollow. "I was so confused, so afraid of what people would think. But Gaspard helped me understand that love isn't something to be ashamed of."

Every word is a dagger in my chest because I know how much it costs her to say them. The Madeline I knew would never speak such lies willingly. This is what he's reduced her to... a puppet mouthing his words.

The speech ends, and they begin to descend from the platform. I push closer, desperate for just a moment of eye contact, some sign that the woman I love is still in there somewhere.

Security is thick around them, but I manage to get within twenty feet before they reach their car. Madeline glances up, scanning the crowd with that same empty expression, and then her eyes find mine.

For an instant, her mask slips. I see recognition flicker across her features, followed by something that might be hope, or maybe just desperate longing. Her lips part slightly, as if she might call out, but then Gaspard's hand is on her elbow, guiding her into the car.

Our eyes hold for one more second before the car door closes between us.

I stand there, frozen, as their vehicle pulls away, my heart pounding so hard I think it might burst. She's alive. She saw me. And in that brief moment of connection, I felt the woman I love reaching out across the impossible distance between us.

"You're him, aren't you?"

I spin around to find a woman in black standing behind me, her dark hair pulled back severely, her eyes sharp and assessing. Something about her seems familiar, though I can't place where I might have seen her.

"I'm sorry?"

"Antosha Valiquette." She steps closer, lowering her voice. "The one who wants to save her."

Every instinct screams danger, but something in her tone makes me pause. "Who are you?"

"Someone who works very close to the situation." She glances around nervously. "Someone who's seen what that monster does to her when the cameras aren't rolling."

My hands clench into fists. "What do you want?"

"To help you get her out." She presses something into my hand—a small piece of paper. "But we have to be smart about it. One wrong move and he'll kill her, make it look like an accident."

I look down at the paper. It's an address and a time. Tomorrow, 2 PM.

"Why would you help her?"

Her expression grows fierce, protective. "Because she's the only good thing in that house. Because I've watched him destroy her piece by piece, and I can't stand by and do nothing anymore."

Before I can ask anything else, she melts back into the crowd, leaving me standing there with a dozen questions and one small slip of hope.

When I return home, Guillame takes one look at my face and pours two glasses of whiskey.

"You saw her."

"Yes." I accept the glass gratefully, downing half of it in one swallow. "She looks... Uncle, what he's doing to her—"

"I know." He sits across from me, his expression grim. "I've been monitoring the situation. The reports I'm getting aren't encouraging."

I tell him about the woman in black, showing him the address. He studies it carefully.

"This could be a trap," he warns.

"Or it could be our only chance." I finish my drink and set the glass down with determination. "I'm going."

"We're going," he corrects. "If this is legitimate, we'll need to move quickly. But Antosha..." He fixes me with a stern look. "Whatever we learn tomorrow, whatever opportunity presents itself, we can't let emotion drive our decisions. Madeline's life depends on us being smart."

I nod, though we both know how difficult that will be. When it comes to her, I'm not sure I can be anything but emotional.

"One more day," I murmur, thinking of her face in that crowd, the brief spark of recognition that told me she hasn't given up completely. "Hold on one more day, *ma petite*. I'm coming for you."

And this time, nothing—not Gaspard's power, not his security, not even the threat of death—will stop me from bringing her home.

11

MADDIE

"Ah, wife." Gaspard stands with his hands on my bare waist, staring at my naked body in the mirror. "I have a gift for you."

I grit my teeth, forcing a smile. "A gift?"

He nods, stepping back to reveal a square velvet box. "A symbol of our union."

My heart sinks as he opens the box, revealing a delicate silver choker with tiny diamonds embedded in the links. My eyes widen as I read the inscription on the outside near the clasp. "Property of G. Malveaux."

Gaspard's fingers brush against my neck as he places it on me and fastens the collar in the back. "Nobody will be able to remove it without this." He holds up a small silver key, dangling it in front of my face before slipping it into his pocket. "You belong to me, *ma souris*."

I swallow hard, my fingers instinctively reaching for the collar. It feels cold and heavy where it rests tight against my skin, a constant reminder of my captivity. "It's... beautiful," I manage to squeak out like the mouse he accuses me of being.

Gaspard's eyes gleam with satisfaction. "I'm glad you like it." He leans in, his lips brushing against my ear. "Now everyone will know you are owned as well, wife."

I force myself to nod, my throat tight with unshed tears. I'm trapped, a prisoner in my own body, and there's nothing I can do to escape. The collar is a constant reminder of my status, a symbol of Gaspard's ownership.

I try to focus on something else, anything else, but the weight of the collar is impossible to ignore. It digs into my skin, a physical and constant reminder of Gaspard's control. I take a deep breath, trying to steady myself, but it's no use. I'm drowning, suffocating under the weight of my despair.

"Turn around, *ma souris*. Let me see how it looks."

I stand and face him, the weight of the collar settling against my skin. It's heavier than it appears, the diamonds catching the light. The metal feels like a shackle, cold and unyielding. I lift my hand to touch it, and he catches my wrist.

"Careful. You wouldn't want to damage it." He releases me and steps closer, his voice dropping to that intimate tone that makes my skin crawl. "There will be no question about where your loyalties lie."

I force my voice to remain steady. "No, Sir. Thank you."

He nods. "Every event, every public appearance, people will see this celebration of our love." His hand traces the edge of the choker, and I suppress a shudder. "And who knows? Perhaps soon we'll have another reason to celebrate; a boy to carry on the family name."

My stomach clenches. The thought of being pregnant again, of bringing another innocent life into this nightmare, fills me with terror.

"Perhaps," I manage, though the word is meaningless in the face of a man who will do anything to make it happen.

He studies my face, and I know he's looking for signs of enthusiasm I can't manufacture. After a moment, he nods.

"Time will tell. But for now, this will serve as a reminder." His thumb brushes over the inscription. "You are mine, *ma souris*. Heart, body, and soul. And soon you'll give me the son I desire."

I close my eyes briefly, sending up a desperate prayer that such a thing never comes to pass. When I open them again, his expression has shifted to something almost tender, a look that would fool anyone who didn't know the monster behind it.

"Now then, let's go see our daughter."

The walk to the nursery feels endless, the choker a constant reminder with every step. When we reach Emilie's room, I'm surprised to find her awake, lying on her back in the crib and making soft cooing sounds.

She's grown so much in the past month. Her dark hair has thickened, and her eyes are starting to show hints of brown. When she sees me approach, her whole face lights up, and she kicks her legs excitedly.

"Hello, my darling," I whisper, reaching down to stroke her cheek. She turns toward my touch, her tiny hand grasping at my finger.

"She's developing well," Gaspard observes, though his tone is clinical rather than warm. "The nurses say she's ahead of most children her age."

I want to pick her up, to hold her against my chest and breathe in that sweet baby scent, but I know better than to ask. Instead, I content myself with touching her soft skin, marveling at how alert she's become. She tracks my movement with her eyes now, and when I smile at her, she responds with what might be her first real smile.

"She recognizes me," I say softly.

"Of course she does. You're her mother." There's something in his tone that suggests he views this connection as temporary, something to be managed and controlled like everything else in this house.

Emilie makes a happy gurgling sound and reaches for the collar at my throat, her fingers fascinated by the sparkle of the diamonds. I lean closer so she can touch it, and she grabs onto it with surprising strength.

"Careful," Gaspard warns. "She's stronger than she looks."

As if to prove his point, Emilie tugs on the choker, and the metal bites into my neck. But I don't pull away. This is the longest I've been able to interact with her in weeks, and I'll endure any discomfort for these precious moments.

"She's perfect," I breathe, smoothing down her soft hair.

"Yes, she is." Gaspard checks his watch. "And that's enough for now. You have duties to attend to."

The dismissal stings, but I've learned not to argue. I lean down and press a gentle kiss to Emilie's forehead, whispering, "Mama loves you, sweetheart."

As we leave the nursery, the weight of the collar seems to increase with every step. It's more than jewelry; it's a brand, a claim, a constant reminder that in Gaspard's eyes, I'm no different from any other possession he owns.

But as I think of Emilie's smile, her bright eyes and grasping fingers, I hold onto the one truth he can never change: I am her mother, and that bond is stronger than any chain he can place around my neck.

THE NURSE'S WORDS HIT ME LIKE A PHYSICAL blow.

"I'm sorry, but those are Mr. Malveaux's orders. Emilie is to be switched to formula immediately, and you're to stop pumping."

I stare at her, certain I've misunderstood. "What do you mean? She's been doing fine with breast milk. There's no reason to change."

"I'm afraid it's not my decision." The nurse, a different one from usual, avoids my eyes. "Mr. Malveaux feels it's time for the transition."

My hands shake as I set down the breast pump. "But I should be able to feed my own child. That's... it's my job. It's what mothers do."

"I understand your concerns, but—"

"No, you don't understand." The words come out sharper than I intended, months of suppressed frustration finally finding a voice. "This is my daughter. She came from my body. It's my fucking choice about how to feed her."

The nurse takes a step back, clearly uncomfortable with my tone. "Mrs. Malveaux, perhaps you should discuss this with your husband—"

"I'll do exactly that."

But before I can move toward the door, it opens, and Gaspard enters with that measured stride that always precedes trouble.

"Is there a problem here?" His voice is calm, yet I can see the steel beneath the surface.

"Yes, there is." I turn to face him, my heart pounding but my resolve firm. "I want to continue breastfeeding Emilie. There's no reason to stop."

His eyebrows rise slightly. "No reason? I think there are several reasons, actually."

"Such as?"

"Such as the fact that you're needed for other duties now that you're appearing publicly with me. Such as the importance of establishing routines that don't revolve entirely around your... biological functions." His tone grows colder with each word as he leans in. "Such as the simple fact that when I make a decision about this household, it's not open for debate."

The nurse edges toward the door, clearly wanting to escape what's becoming an argument. Gaspard notices and nods toward her.

"Leave us."

She hurries out, and I'm alone with him, my defiance suddenly feeling much more precarious.

"Maddie." His voice drops to that dangerous quiet that I've learned to fear. "Did you think you could countermand my orders? In front of the staff?"

"I thought I could ask questions about my own daughter's care."

"Your daughter." He laughs, but there's no humor in it. "Our daughter, *ma souris*. And in this house, I make the decisions about what's best for our family."

I want to back down, to apologize and retreat to the safety of compliance. But the image of Emilie's trusting face fills my mind, and I find strength I didn't know I still possessed.

"She's thriving on breast milk. All doctors recommend—"

"Shut up. I have the final say, not the doctors, no matter what is recommended." He steps closer, and I force myself not to retreat even though I do flinch at his tone. "I'm telling you that this discussion is over. You will stop pumping. You will accept the formula feeding schedule. And you will never again question my decisions in front of the staff."

"But—"

The word dies in my throat as his hand shoots out, gripping my chin hard enough to leave marks.

"What did I say about questioning my decisions?"

I can barely breathe, let alone speak. The collar around my neck seems to tighten, a physical reminder of exactly how powerless I am in this situation. I know the true reason he wants me to quit breastfeeding and it has to do with only *one* duty—my ability to get pregnant again.

"I'm sorry," I whisper.

"Sorry for what?"

"Sorry for questioning you. Sorry for... for thinking I have the right to make decisions."

His grip loosens slightly. "Better. Now, you'll go with the nurse for your examination. And you'll remember this conversation the next time you're tempted to overstep your bounds."

He releases me and steps back, his expression returning to that mask of calm control. "The nurse is waiting in the medical room."

I nod and head for the door, my chin throbbing where his fingers pressed too hard. As I walk down the hallway, I think about Emilie's bright eyes and eager smile, and I wonder how many other small freedoms he'll strip away in the name of control.

By the time I reach the medical room, I've made a silent promise to my daughter: I may have lost this battle, but I won't stop fighting for her. Somehow, someday, I'll find a way to give her the life she deserves.

Even if it costs me everything.

12

MADDIE

THE PREGNANCY TEST IS NEGATIVE.

I felt relief upon seeing the results, but Gaspard's expression tells me that my reprieve will come at a cost. His jaw tightens as he stares at the results, and when he finally looks at me, his eyes are cold with disappointment.

"Unacceptable," he says quietly. "Two months we've been trying, *ma souris*."

I sit on my bed, hands folded in my lap. There's nothing I can say that won't make this worse, but I manage to whisper, "I'm sorry, Sir. I don't control nature."

"Perhaps you need a reminder of what's expected of you as my wife. Get up!" he roars, his voice amplifying, echoing off the walls, and reverberating through my very bones. I obey mindlessly, my legs trembling as I push myself off the bed. Gaspard's gaze sweeps over me, scrutinizing every inch of my body, his expression a clear reflection of his disappointment.

"You've displeased me today," he snarls, the words laced with disdain before the corners of his slips curl in a cruel smile. "But don't worry, wife. I'll have another child to hold soon enough."

I remain silent, biting my tongue to hold back the words that threaten to spill out. There are tears pricking at the corners of my eyes, yet I refuse to let them fall. I won't give him the satisfaction of seeing me break.

He moves towards me, his steps deliberate and menacing. Instinctively, I retreat, my heart hammering against my ribcage. His towering figure looms over me, casting a long, dark shadow that engulfs me, making me feel like a trapped animal, cornered and helpless.

"You understand what comes next, don't you?" he asks, his voice as cold as ice.

I shake my head in denial, refusing to acknowledge the cruel insinuation lurking behind his words. My breath hitches as he seizes my arm, his fingers biting into my flesh with a punishing grip. I stifle a cry of pain, but don't dare attempt to break free from his hold.

Removing my dress in one swift motion, he leaves me completely exposed and vulnerable. His eyes rake over my naked body, and a shiver of revulsion crawls up my spine.

"Grab the bedpost," he commands, his voice devoid of any warmth or humanity.

Oh, god.

My body goes rigid as he pulls his leather belt free from its loops, the sound of it slicing through the air making my heart race. He folds it in half with a menacing snap, his eyes never leaving mine. With a guttural snarl, he shoves me towards the bedpost, and I scramble to avoid hitting my face against the hard wood. Instead, I wrap my arms around it, turning my face to the side and hiding it in the protective crook of my shoulder.

It's been a while since he last hit me, and every fiber of my being is braced for the worst. And I'm proven right when the first smack lands across my back, a searing line of pain that makes me gasp.

"Count!" His voice is harsh and commanding.

Yet, I can't bring myself to do as he wants, or acknowledge the pain he's inflicting. Each strike of the belt is a sharp reminder of his control, his power over me. He hits me again, and again, the sound echoing in the room like a sickening drumbeat. His fingers tangle in my hair, yanking my head back so hard I feel a sharp pain in my scalp.

"I said count," he snarls, releasing me again to continue the assault.

Somehow, some way, I've retreated into myself even though I manage to count like he asks. The belt slaps against my skin, no doubt painting a brutal picture of bruises across my back, my ass, and my thighs. But I've disconnected from my body, as if I'm floating above myself, watching this horrifying scene unfold. Tears stream down my face, hot and silent, but I don't feel the pain anymore. I'm numb, detached, freed from the pain he inflicts even as I'm trapped in an impossible nightmare.

I lose track of time as the belt continues to rain down on me, each strike a blur of pain that I somehow manage to push away. The only clarity comes when my fingers, slick with sweat, slip off the bedpost. I'm falling, the plush carpet rushing up to meet me, but then, suddenly, I'm caught. His arms, the same ones that inflicted this torment, encircle me, holding me up as if I'm fragile, precious. The irony is not lost on me, and it twists my stomach into knots.

Gaspard puts down on the bed and rests beside me, his hand surprisingly gentle as he strokes my hair.

"This hurts me more than it hurts you," he murmurs, though we both know that's a lie. "But you must understand disappointing me has consequences. Failing to give me what I need has consequences."

"Eva will tend to you in the morning," he finally says when I remain silent, covering me with a blanket. "And next time you won't fail me, will you?"

I shake my head because it's the only response that won't make this worse.

"Good girl." He presses a kiss to my forehead, and the contrast between his gentle lips and the fire across my back makes my stomach lurch. "I have a meeting to attend to. Rest, recover, and remember —I only discipline you because I love you."

It's the last thing I remember him saying before I fall into a fitful sleep, my back on fire and my eyes wanting to shed tears that for some reason won't fall.

I CATCH MY REFLECTION IN THE BATHROOM mirror and wince at what I see. The welts across my back have darkened overnight, angry purple lines that stand out starkly against my pale skin. Every movement sends fresh waves of pain through my body, but I've learned to hide it well.

The collar glints at my throat, a constant

reminder of ownership that feels even more suffocating this morning. I touch it gently, feeling the raised letters of his name against my fingertips.

A soft knock at the door startles me. "Come in."

Eva enters the room, and I stare at her while tears stream down my cheeks because he's continued to gag her. Her eyes flick to the mirror and widen in horror at the sight of what Gaspard has done.

Even though I want to hug her, tell her how much I miss her, I don't. I am out of energy and can take no more pain today so my voice is flat as I ask the question. I know she's supposed to be here since Gaspard said so last night and I stare at her, waiting for her to do whatever she's come to do.

She holds up a jar of something in her hand, and points at me before moving her hand to indicate I should lay on the bed. She follows me over and makes it clear with motions that I am to be on my stomach as she shows me the jar.

It is an ointment meant to ease the discomfort of Gaspard's punishment. He wanted to make sure I got the message, but he doesn't want my skin marked permanently. I'm too vital to his humble family man image to leave anything like that for someone to discover.

As Eva smoothes my back with the ointment, I say nothing. If he is listening somehow, I don't want to give him any more ammo, no matter how much I miss my friend.

I close my eyes, letting out a slow breath as the cool ointment touches my battered skin. Eva's gentle touch is a balm to my soul, and for a moment, I forget about the hell I'm living in.

But as I relax, there is sudden wetness on my back, and my eyes snap open. I realize Eva is crying, her tears dripping onto my skin as she continues to tend to my wounds. My heart goes out to her; she's been gagged, silenced, and forced to watch me suffer. I can only imagine the helplessness she feels in the face of what Gaspard's doing to us.

"Eva," I whisper, my voice barely audible. I reach back, hesitant to touch her because it's definitely not allowed.

She looks up, her eyes red-rimmed, and her desperation is clear. She wants to help me, to get me out of this nightmare, but she's trapped too.

As she finishes, she rubs her hand on her skirt, and then reaches out to cup my face. "Ummm mmmm mmm. Mm mmm."

I don't know what she's trying to say, but the kindness in her touch makes my eyes tear up. "I love you," I whisper to her, thankful for the brief contact we've had tonight. "I miss you."

She nods, rubbing her thumb on my cheek for a

second before sliding off the bed, and leaves me alone moments later. I don't know why Gaspard let her come in here this morning; if I didn't know any better, I would think he felt guilty for causing me so much pain that I nearly passed out. However, it's more likely he wanted to show me again what he can do and take from me.

But every time he mistreats me, or keeps me from my baby, or throws his power in my face, all it does is make me angrier.

He thinks I won't run again if given the chance, but he's wrong. I'll wait for the right moment and the instant I have the opportunity, I'm taking it. At least if he does kill me, I'll have died trying to get the fuck out of here.

13

―――

ANTOSHA

THE ADDRESS LEADS ME TO A SMALL CAFÉ ON the outskirts of the city, the kind of place where conversations can be held in relative privacy. Guillame insisted on coming despite my protests, and now we sit at a corner table, both of us scanning the room for anyone who might be watching.

At exactly two o'clock, a woman in her forties enters, her graying hair pulled back in a neat bun. She's dressed simply but professionally. Her eyes sweep the room until they find us, and she approaches with measured steps.

"Mr. Valiquette?" Her voice is quiet but steady.

"Yes." I stand, offering her the chair across from us. "And you are?"

"Claire. I'm one of the nurses who cares for..."

She pauses, glancing around the café. "For the baby."

My heart clenches at the mention of the baby. "How is she? How is Madeline?"

Claire's expression grows grim. "That's why I'm here. What he's doing to her... it's getting worse."

Guillame leans forward. "How did you know to contact us?"

"Eva. The girl who helps care for Mrs. Malveaux. She's desperate to help but can't leave the house easily. She asked me to find you." Claire's hands tremble slightly as she reaches for the coffee cup I've ordered for her. "She said you tried to protect Madeline before. That you might try again."

"We will," I say without hesitation. "Tell us what you know."

Claire takes a shaky breath. "The house is like a fortress. Guards everywhere, cameras, electronic locks on most doors. But there are patterns, routines. Malveaux has his schedule, and so does the security."

"What about Madeline? Where is she kept?"

"She has some freedom to move around the house during the day, but at night..." Claire's face darkens. "At night she's locked in his bedroom. And lately, he's been punishing her more frequently. For not getting pregnant again."

My hands clench into fists on the table. Guillame places a warning hand on my arm.

"The baby?" Guillame asks.

"Beautiful little girl and healthy. But she's kept in a separate nursery with round-the-clock care. Madeline only gets to see her for short periods, and never alone." Claire wipes at her eyes. "It's heartbreaking watching a mother be kept from her child like that."

"Security detail?" I force myself to focus on logistics rather than my rage.

"Changes shifts every eight hours. Fewer guards on duty between midnight and six AM, but the house is locked down tight then. Electronic surveillance is lighter during his campaign events— more focus on external security."

"Campaign events," Guillame muses. "When is the next one?"

"Next Thursday evening. A fundraising gala at the Grand Hotel. He'll want Madeline there, playing the devoted wife." Claire's voice turns bitter. "She hates those events, but she has no choice."

I lean forward. "What about staff? Who can we trust?"

"Eva, definitely. She loves Madeline like a sister, but she's watched constantly. There's one guard, Marcus, who seems... different. Kinder. Eva thinks he might be sympathetic, but we can't be sure."

"And you? Why are you willing to help?"

Claire's expression hardens. "Because I became a nurse to help people, not to enable monsters. What he does to her, what I've seen..." She shakes her head. "I have daughters of my own. I can't stand by and watch this continue."

Guillame and I exchange glances. This woman is genuine; I can see it in her eyes, hear it in her voice.

"What do you need from us?" she asks.

"Information. Schedules, layouts, anything you can provide without raising suspicion." I lean back, my mind already working through possibilities. "And communication. We need a way to let Madeline know we're coming."

"I can pass along messages. Malveaux watches everyone's interactions closely, but I'm usually alone with Maddie and the baby."

"Tell her..." I pause, thinking of what would mean something to Madeline without being obvious to anyone else. "Tell her that someone remembers the chess lessons. That the student is still learning the game."

Claire nods, though she looks confused. "Chess lessons?"

"She'll understand."

We spend another thirty minutes going over details—guard rotations, the layout of the house, Malveaux's habits. When Claire finally stands to leave, she presses a folded paper into my hand.

"Floor plans of the house. Eva managed to sketch them from memory. Good luck."

After she's gone, Guillame and I sit in silence for several minutes.

"It's possible," he finally says. "Difficult, dangerous, but possible."

"When?"

"Not the gala. Too public, too many variables. But we can use it to our advantage, like scout security and confirm patterns." He studies the floor plans Claire left behind. "We need more preparation time. More information."

"How long?"

"A few weeks. Maybe a month."

"She might not have a month," I say quietly, thinking of Claire's description of increasing punishments.

"And if we rush this and fail, she'll definitely not have a month." Guillame folds the papers carefully. "I understand your urgency, nephew. But dead heroes save no one."

I know he's right, but the knowledge doesn't ease the burning need to act immediately. Somewhere across the city, the woman I love is suffering, and every day we delay is another day of hell for her.

But as we leave the café and head back to begin serious planning, I hold onto one thought: for the first time in months, rescue isn't just a desperate hope.

It's a real possibility.

And I'll move heaven and earth to make it happen.

THE DRIVE BACK TO THE ESTATE PASSES IN tense silence, both Guillame and I lost in our own thoughts. When we finally reach the house, I head straight for my old room—the one I occupied before my disastrous marriage—and spread Claire's sketched floor plans across the desk.

The layout is more complex than I remembered from our brief time sheltering Madeline. Multiple wings, countless rooms, and what appears to be a newer section added to the back of the house. Claire's notes are written in careful script alongside Eva's drawings: "Master bedroom—locked at night," "Nursery—24hr guard," "Kitchen entrance—delivery schedule."

I study every detail, committing guard positions and patrol routes to memory. The main challenge isn't getting into the house—it's getting Madeline and Emilie out alive. Malveaux isn't the type to simply let us walk away with what he considers his property.

A soft knock interrupts my planning. "Come in."

Léonie enters, looking hesitant in a way that's unusual for her. Since our annulment, our interactions have been cordial but distant—two people who shared a brief, unwanted marriage and are now trying to navigate friendship.

"I heard you went out today," she says, settling into the chair across from my desk.

"Yes." I don't elaborate, but she notices the papers spread before me.

"This is about her, isn't it? The girl."

There's no point in denying it. "Her name is Madeline."

"I know her name." Léonie leans forward, studying the floor plans with sharp eyes. "And I know you're planning something incredibly dangerous."

"Probably."

She's quiet for a long moment, then surprises me by asking, "What do you need?"

I look up from the sketches. "What?"

"You heard me. What do you need? Money? Resources? A distraction?" Her expression is serious, determined. "That man is a monster, Antosha. What he did to her when she lived here, what he's doing to her now... I may not have loved you as a wife should, but I care about you as a friend. And no friend of mine should have to watch the woman he loves suffer."

The unexpected offer of help catches me off guard. "Léonie, this could be dangerous. If Malveaux discovers you're involved—"

"Let me worry about that." She stands and moves to the window, gazing out at the grounds where Madeline once walked. "Besides, my family has resources he doesn't know about. Contacts in places that might prove useful."

"Such as?"

A small smile plays at her lips. "Did you know my cousin works for the city's emergency services? He's the one who coordinates ambulance dispatches."

The implication hits me immediately. "A medical emergency could provide cover for entering the house."

"Exactly. And if there were multiple emergencies happening simultaneously across the city, it might draw security resources away from other locations."

I stare at her, seeing my old friend in a new light. "Why would you do this?"

"Because that girl trusted us to keep her safe, and we failed her." Léonie's voice grows fierce. "Because she has a child who deserves better than growing up in that house. And because..." She pauses, looking almost embarrassed. "Because I've seen how you've been these past months. You're miserable, Antosha. You barely eat, barely sleep. You're wasting away from guilt and longing."

"I'm fine—"

"You're not fine. You haven't been fine since the day she was taken." Léonie returns to her chair, leaning forward earnestly. "I want my friend back. The man who used to laugh, who used to find joy in simple things. And if saving her is what it takes to bring that man back, then I'll help you do it."

The generosity of her offer, especially after everything our forced marriage put her through, leaves me speechless for a moment.

"The risks—"

"Are worth it." She reaches across the desk and covers my hand with hers. "Just promise me you won't get yourself killed trying to be a hero. Plan carefully, be smart about this."

"Guillame said the same thing."

"Then listen to us. We both care about you too much to lose you to noble stupidity." She stands to leave, then pauses at the door. "And Antosha? When you rescue her, because I believe you will, bring her home. She belongs here, with people who will protect her properly this time."

After she leaves, I return to studying the floor plans with renewed focus. Now I'm not just planning a rescue—I'm planning a homecoming. Claire's sketches suddenly look less like an impossible fortress and more like a puzzle to be solved.

I pull out a fresh sheet of paper and begin outlining our approach. Phase one: reconnaissance during the gala. Phase two: establish communication with Eva. Phase three: execution.

Somewhere in that house, Madeline is enduring another night of captivity. But if Claire is right about the patterns, if Eva can provide inside assistance, if Léonie's resources can create the right distractions...

For the first time since watching her disappear into Malveaux's car, I allow myself to believe that bringing her home isn't just a dream.

It's an ending that I refuse to fail to achieve.

14

MADDIE

THE NURSERY FEELS LIKE A SANCTUARY DURING my precious hour with Emilie. At four months old, she's become so much more aware of the world around her, her bright eyes tracking my movements as I approach her crib.

"Hello, my beautiful girl," I whisper, lifting her into my arms. She's heavier now, more solid, and when she sees my face, she rewards me with one of those gummy smiles that makes my heart ache with love.

Emilie babbles softly, her tiny hands reaching for the collar at my throat. I let her touch the cold metal, hating that she's becoming familiar with this symbol of my captivity. Her fingers are stronger now, grasping with more purpose, and she manages to wrap them around one of the diamonds.

"Gentle, sweetheart," I murmur, carefully extracting her fingers before she can pull too hard.

The night nurse watches from across the room with a soft expression. She's been kind during these visits, giving me space to bond with my daughter while remaining close enough to intervene if required.

"She's grown so much this week," the nurse says quietly, moving closer. "Her neck control is excellent for her age."

"She's perfect," I breathe, settling into the rocking chair with Emilie against my chest. The baby immediately snuggles into me, her tiny fist curling in my dress.

"She knows you're her mama," she observes. "See how she relaxes in your arms? That's pure recognition and trust."

The words make tears spring to my eyes. Despite all of Gaspard's efforts to control every aspect of our lives, this bond remains unbroken.

As we rock gently, Emilie making soft cooing sounds, the nurse begins tidying the already spotless nursery. Her movements bring her closer to my chair, and when she leans down to adjust Emilie's blanket, she whispers so quietly I almost miss it.

"Someone remembers the chess lessons. The student is still learning the game."

My heart stops. Chess lessons. Only two people would phrase it that way, would remember me learning to play during those precious weeks of freedom.

Antosha and Guillame.

They're out there. They remember. They haven't forgotten about me.

I force myself to remain calm, to keep rocking as if nothing has changed, but inside, something that has been dormant for months suddenly sparks to life. Hope. After all this time, someone is still fighting for me.

"Did you hear me?" The nurse asks in a normal voice, straightening up. "I said she's due for her feeding soon."

"Yes," I manage, my voice only slightly unsteady. "I heard you."

The nurse nods and moves away, but not before I catch the meaningful look in her eyes. She's not just a nurse; she's an ally. Then she returns with a warm bottle and hands it to me.

For the rest of my time with Emilie, I hold her closer and feed her, hating that she's suckling on a bottle and not at my breast, which has dried up now.

When I kiss her forehead, whispering that we're going to get out of here no matter what,

Emilie responds with a happy gurgle, as if she understands that everything is about to change.

When my hour is up and I have to return her to the crib, I press a long kiss to her forehead. "I love you, my darling girl. More than you'll ever know."

As I leave the nursery, the collar feels lighter around my neck. Gaspard can chain my body, control my movements, punish my defiance. But he can't touch the flame of hope that's been rekindled in my chest.

Someone remembers. Someone is coming.

And for the first time in months, I believe there might actually be an ending to this fucking nightmare I'm trapped in.

THE SMALL WHITE STICK IN MY HAND SHOWS two clear pink lines, and my stomach drops to the floor.

"Excellent," Gaspard says from behind me, satisfaction evident in his voice. "Right on schedule."

I stare at the ovulation test, my hands trembling. He's been making me take these daily for the past week, monitoring my cycle with the precision of a scientist. The positive result means my body is primed for conception which is exactly what he's been waiting for.

"Sir," I begin, but he cuts me off with a raised hand.

"No excuses tonight, *ma souris*. As if I would allow you any." His eyes gleam with anticipation. "Tonight, you give me a son."

The thought of another child conceived in violence, raised in this house of horrors, makes me want to vomit. But I know better than to show my revulsion.

"Of course," I whisper.

"Good girl." He moves closer, his hand settling possessively on my waist. "I've already instructed the staff that we're not to be disturbed. Tonight is about our family's future."

I close my eyes as he leads me toward the bedroom, trying to retreat into that safe place in my mind where his touch can't reach me. But the spark of hope the nurse's message ignited makes it harder to disconnect completely. Someone is coming for me, but will they arrive in time?

"You seem distracted," Gaspard observes as he begins unbuttoning his shirt. "I hope you're not having second thoughts about your duties as a wife."

"No, Sir. I'm just... thinking about Emilie. How she'll adjust to having a brother or sister."

The lie comes easily, and he accepts it with a pleased nod.

"Family is everything." He moves to the dresser. "But first, we need to ensure conception occurs."

My throat tightens.

Gaspard carries over a small leather case and sets it on the bed with deliberate care. My pulse spikes when he withdraws two silk ties, folding them neatly as though this were a formal ritual rather than a violation.

"Your body belongs to me," he murmurs, eyes gleaming as he holds the ties up, "and tonight it fulfills its purpose. We'll keep at it until I'm certain you're carrying my son."

From the case he produces a slim syringe filled with a pale liquid. He holds it up to the light, flicking the barrel in a way that makes my stomach twist.

"A little encouragement," he says almost cheerfully, as though he's offering me champagne instead of hormones. "Perhaps it will bless us with twins this time."

I bite the inside of my cheek until I taste copper, forcing myself not to react, not to shudder at the thought of bringing two more innocent lives into his world.

He sets the syringe on the nightstand, as casual

as if it were a fountain pen, and begins rolling up his sleeves. My skin crawls at the ritual of it with his careful preparation and the anticipation in his eyes. He savors every step, not because it's necessary, but because he knows I'm watching.

"Undress," he commands. The word cracks like a whip.

My fingers fumble at the buttons of my dress, but I keep my face smooth, empty. If I let him see fear, it will only feed him. Instead I think of Emilie asleep in the nursery and of the nurse's words that have given me hope that soon I'll be away from this disgusting man.

He comes closer, the silk ties draped across his hand. When he brushes them against my wrist, I force myself not to recoil. To him, they're tools of devotion, binding me to his will. To me, they're shackles but also proof. He's afraid of losing control, or he wouldn't need to tie me down.

"You're quiet tonight," he observes, studying me as if silence itself were rebellion.

"I'm focused, Sir," I whisper, letting the lie slip easily from my lips. "For our family's future."

He smiles, sharp and satisfied. "Good girl."

Inside, I bury myself deeper in that small ember of hope. Someone is coming. Someone knows. If I can just endure tonight — one more ritual, one more cycle — then maybe the ties won't hold me forever.

He ties my hands together, then once I'm in the position he wants me on the bed, he connects them to the bedpost, so they are above my head. Putting a pillow beneath my hips, he spreads my legs wide, almost unbearably so.

"Don't move or you'll be punished." I feel him wipe down a fleshy part of my hip right by my ass, then there's a poke from the needle, which makes me gasp while he laughs low. "Excellent. Now, let's make sure your body is ready to receive my seed."

His use of that word makes me want to fucking gag. But I know what's next. He's going to warm me up, make sure I'm on the verge of an orgasm so when he ejaculates, my body will 'do its job' properly.

The next hour passes by so slowly. Tears silently slip down my cheeks as he forces my body to respond and as I orgasm, he shoves his way in, forcefully raping me and making me scream from his harsh pace until he comes.

He does this not once, but twice, and leaves me tied in with my hips raised, legs spread. He puts a familiar bar thing between my legs, keeping my legs spread and preventing me from sleeping comfortably in any other position. Then, he prepares for bed, forcing a deep kiss on me after he shuts off the lights and rolls over to sleep.

I lie staring at the ceiling unable to do anything except hope his attempts didn't take, my arms aching from their forced position which will probably prevent me from resting well.

So I focus on something else: the nurse's message about the chess lessons.

Guillame taught me that chess requires patience, strategy, and the ability to think several moves ahead. Sometimes you have to sacrifice pieces to achieve a larger goal. Sometimes the game looks hopeless until the very last move.

I pray again that no new life has begun there tonight, while simultaneously holding onto the hope that rescue might come before it matters.

The collar at my throat catches the moonlight streaming through the window, a constant reminder of my captivity. But tonight, it doesn't feel quite as heavy as before.

Because somewhere out there, someone is planning their next move in this deadly game.

And I'm going to be ready when they make it.

15

MADDIE

"*Ma souris...*"

I wake to Gaspard's body sliding on top of mine as he whispers in my ear, his hand between my legs priming my body once more. I'm barely awake he takes advantage of my body once more.

Luckily it's quicker this morning, and when he rolls off me, it's with a content sigh. He goes to the bathroom first, then when he returns, he's got some something in his hands. Doesn't even tell me what it is before reaching again between my legs, and I gasp from the pain as he pushes it deep inside me.

Tears prick my eyes as he then slides my underwear back on, pulling the pillow out from under me once done. They hold whatever he's put inside me in place and after he's done untying my wrists, he says softly, "Sit up."

I move quickly to comply, noting his unusually

calm tone. Whatever he's planning, I don't want to give him any reason to become violent.

"You'll go to the restroom, be careful to keep the plug in, understand?" When I nod, he continues. "Tonight is the fundraising gala. You'll be playing the devoted wife for all our important guests."

My heart sinks. Another public performance, another night of pretending to love the man who's destroyed my life, all while trying to walk normally with this uncomfortable plug inside me.

"Yes, Sir," I manage.

"I've had something special made for the occasion." He gets up, walks to the closet, and gets out a dress. It is a deep emerald green that I know will complement the collar perfectly. "You'll look stunning. The perfect political wife."

The irony makes me sick. To everyone at that gala, I'll appear to be living a fairy tale; the young woman who found love with her stepfather after tragedy brought them together. They'll never see the bruises hidden on my backside beneath the elegant fabric, never know about the prison I return to each night.

"Eva will help you prepare this afternoon," he continues, laying the dress carefully on the bed. "Hair, makeup, everything must be perfect. This is an important night for my campaign."

"Of course." I keep my voice steady, though inside I'm calculating. A public event means crowds, distractions, security focused outward rather than inward. If the Valiquette men are truly planning something...

"You seem more cooperative today, *ma souris*," Gaspard observes, studying my face. "I'm pleased. Perhaps last night reminded you of your priorities."

I nod, not trusting my voice. Let him think I've been broken by his latest cruelty. Let him believe I've given up hope.

"Excellent. Now rest. Tonight will be a long evening, and I need you at your best." He moves toward the door, then pauses. "Oh, and Maddie? Remember that everyone will be watching tonight. Every gesture, every expression will be scrutinized. Don't disappoint me."

After he leaves, I remain sitting on the bed, my mind racing. Tonight. If rescue is coming, tonight might be the perfect opportunity.

Or it might be the night that seals my fate forever.

THE GRAND HOTEL BALLROOM GLITTERS WITH crystal chandeliers and the sparkle of expensive jewelry. I stand beside Gaspard, my hand resting on his arm as he greets donor after donor, my smile never wavering despite the exhaustion weighing down my limbs.

The emerald dress fits perfectly, as I knew it would. Gaspard's eye for detail ensures that every aspect of my appearance serves his political image. The collar catches the light beautifully, drawing admiring glances from women who see it as an extravagant gift rather than the chain it truly is.

"Madeline, you look radiant," gushes Mrs. Fontaine, a prominent society wife whose husband contributes heavily to Gaspard's campaigns. "Marriage certainly agrees with you."

"Thank you," I reply graciously. "Gaspard takes excellent care of me."

The lie flows smoothly from my lips after months of practice. Gaspard's hand tightens approvingly on mine as he launches into a discussion about municipal infrastructure with her husband.

I let the conversation wash over me, my eyes scanning the crowded ballroom. Somewhere in this sea of formally dressed guests, are Antosha's eyes on me? Is he here, watching, planning?

"Excuse me," I murmur during a brief lull. "I need to powder my nose."

Gaspard's grip on my arm tightens because he can't very well stop me from going to the bathroom in front of all these people. "Of course, darling. But don't be long."

His tone is light, but the warning is clear. I have a short leash, even here.

The ladies' room is thankfully empty when I enter, giving me a moment to breathe without performing. I stare at my reflection in the ornate mirror—pale skin, dark circles artfully concealed with makeup, and that damned collar glinting against my throat.

The door opens behind me, and I expect to see another guest. Instead, a tall figure in an expensive tuxedo enters, closing the door quietly behind him.

My breath catches. "Antosha."

He looks different—older, more worn than I remember. But his eyes are the same, filled with that intensity that used to make my heart race for entirely different reasons.

"*Ma petite*," he breathes, taking a step toward me before stopping himself. "God, what has he done to you?"

I want to run to him, to collapse into his arms and let him carry me away from this nightmare. But I know better.

"You can't be here," I whisper urgently. "How did you even get in? If someone sees—"

"I had to see you, snuck in through the back

where there is less security. I needed to tell you we're working on getting you out."

Hope flares in my chest, bright and desperate. "When? Tonight?"

His expression grows pained. "No. Not tonight. The security is too tight, too many variables. We need more time to plan."

The hope crumbles, leaving me feeling more hollow than before. "How much time?"

"A few weeks. Maybe less if we can—"

"I might not have a few weeks." The words come out sharper than I intended. "He's monitoring everything. My cycle, my body. He wants another child, and he won't stop until he gets one."

Antosha's hands clench into fists. "I'm going to kill him."

"No." I step closer, my voice fierce despite its whisper. "You're going to get me and Emilie out of there. Alive. Both of us alive."

"We will. I swear to you, we will." He reaches toward my face, then stops, his hand falling to his side. "The nurse—she's helping us. And Eva. They're gathering information, building a plan."

"Eva?" My heart lifts slightly. At least my friend isn't completely alone in this.

"She loves you. She'd do anything to help." His eyes search mine desperately. "Hold on a little longer. Can you do that?"

I touch the collar at my throat, feeling its weight. "I don't have a choice."

"Yes, you do. You can survive this. You're stronger than he knows, stronger than he'll ever be."

Voices in the hallway make us both freeze.

"I have to go," I whisper.

"Wait." His eyes bore into mine with desperate intensity. "Remember what you learned about chess. Sometimes the weakest piece can become the most powerful. The pawn that makes it across the board."

I nod, understanding the deeper meaning. "I remember."

He moves toward the door, then pauses. "Maddie? I lo—"

"Don't." I shake my head, tears threatening to spill. "Don't say it. Not here. Not like this."

He nods, understanding, and slips out of the room as quietly as he entered.

I stand alone for several minutes, staring at my reflection and trying to compose myself. His words echo in my mind—the pawn that makes it across the board. In chess, that lowly piece can transform into anything: a queen, a rook, a knight. The most powerful transformation on the board.

When I finally return to the ballroom, Gaspard is exactly where I left him, though his eyes narrow slightly as I approach.

"You were gone a while," he observes.

"There was a line," I lie smoothly, slipping my arm through his.

He studies my face for a moment, then nods, apparently satisfied. But for the rest of the evening, his grip on me never loosens, and I notice his security detail watching me more closely than usual.

As we finally leave the hotel, Gaspard's hand possessive on my back, I think about Antosha's words again.

A pawn. The weakest piece on the board.

But as I learned months ago, if a pawn can make it across the board, it can become anything it wants to be.

Even a queen.

And I'm going to make it across this board, no matter what it takes.

16

MADDIE

THE DAYS FOLLOWING THE GALA BLUR together in a haze of careful compliance. I move through the house like a ghost, speaking only when spoken to, doing exactly as I'm told without question or hesitation. Every instinct I have focuses on one thing: survival until rescue comes.

But my newfound docility seems to have the opposite effect on Gaspard than I intended.

"You're like a lifeless doll," he snaps over breakfast, his fork clattering against his plate. "Sitting there with that vacant expression, nodding at everything I say."

I blink, unsure how to respond. Yesterday he punished me for showing too much spirit. Today my obedience angers him.

"I'm sorry, Sir. I thought—"

"You thought what? That acting like a mindless idiot would please me?" He pushes back from the table, his chair scraping harshly against the floor. "I married a woman, not a puppet."

The irony would be laughable if it weren't so terrifying. He's spent months breaking me down, demanding complete submission, and now that he has it, he's disgusted by it.

"What would you like me to do differently, Sir?" I ask carefully.

"I want you to act like you're alive!" His voice echoes off the dining room walls. "Show some emotion, some... fire. The girl I fell in love with had spirit."

The girl he fell in love with. As if what he feels for me could ever be called love. As if I ever had a choice in becoming the object of his obsession.

"I'm trying to be what you want me to be," I say quietly.

"Are you? Because what I see is a woman going through the motions of living while she plans her next escape attempt."

My blood turns to ice. Does he know about the gala? About seeing Antosha?

"I'm not planning anything, Sir. I've learned my lesson."

He studies my face with those cold, calculating

eyes. "Have you? Because you seem... different since the gala. Distant. Like you're hiding something."

I force myself to meet his gaze directly. "I'm not hiding anything. I'm just tired."

"'Tired.'" He repeats the word like it tastes bitter. "Of what, exactly? Your comfortable life? Your beautiful home? Your devoted husband?"

Each word is a small knife, cutting deeper than the last. But I've learned to absorb his cruelty without flinching.

"No, Sir. Physically tired. I haven't been sleeping well."

"And why is that?"

The honest answer, that I lie awake each night reliving Antosha's promise and counting days until rescue might come, would get me beaten. So I give him something else, something closer to a different truth.

"I miss Emilie. I know I only get to see her for an hour each day, but the rest of the time... I worry about her."

Something shifts in his expression, a flicker of what might be understanding. "You're a mother. It's natural to worry."

For a moment, I think I've found safe ground. Then his face hardens again.

"But you need to remember that Emilie is not your only responsibility. You have a duty to me, to our future children. Obsessing over one child while neglecting your other obligations is selfish."

Future children. The thought makes my stomach clench, but I nod as if I agree.

"You're right, Sir. I apologize."

"Better." He returns to his seat, cutting his food with sharp, precise movements. "Tonight, we're dining with the Fontaines. I want you animated, engaging. Show them the woman I married, not this hollow shell you've become."

"Of course."

"And *ma souris*?" He looks up from his plate, his eyes glinting dangerously. "If you embarrass me in front of them, if you sit there like a statue the way you have been, there will be consequences. Am I clear?"

"Yes, Sir."

The rest of breakfast passes in tense silence. When he finally leaves for his office, I remain at the table, my hands shaking as I try to finish my coffee.

This is impossible. When I fight him, he punishes me. When I submit, he's disgusted. When I show emotion, it's the wrong kind. When I'm quiet, I'm too distant. There's no winning with him, no behavior that will keep me safe.

Eva enters to clear the breakfast dishes, her

movements quick and efficient. She can't speak with the gag in place, but I catch her eye and see the concern there. She's noticed the change in Gaspard's behavior too.

As she works, I think about Antosha's words from the gala. Hold on a little longer. But how much longer? And what if Gaspard's frustration with my behavior leads to something worse?

I touch the collar at my throat, feeling its familiar weight. Sometimes the weakest piece can become the most powerful. But right now, I feel weaker than ever, trapped in a game where the rules change without warning and every move I make seems to be the wrong one.

Eva finishes clearing the table and heads toward the kitchen. As she passes my chair, she lets her hand brush against my shoulder... the briefest touch, but it carries a world of comfort.

I'm not alone in this house. Eva cares, the nurse is helping from the outside, and somewhere beyond these walls, Antosha is working to bring me home.

I just have to survive long enough for rescue to arrive. Even if it means navigating Gaspard's increasingly unpredictable moods, even if it means pretending to be whatever version of myself he wants on any given day.

The alternative, giving up hope, isn't an option.

Not when my daughter needs me to be strong.

Not when freedom might be just weeks away.

THE AFTERNOON STRETCHES ENDLESSLY AS I try to prepare for dinner. Gaspard's demands echo in my mind: animated, engaging, the woman he married. But I can barely remember who that person was supposed to be.

I stand before my closet, staring at the array of dresses he's chosen for me over the months. Each one carefully selected to project the right image— the devoted wife, the perfect political partner, the woman who chose love over convention.

All lies, but lies I have to sell convincingly tonight.

Eva appears in the doorway, carrying a small tray with tea. She's still gagged, but her eyes hold a question as she looks between me and the dresses.

"The blue one, I think," I say softly, pointing to a navy dress that strikes the right balance between elegant and approachable. "Mrs. Fontaine apparently likes classic styles."

Eva nods and retrieves the dress, laying it carefully on the bed. As she pours my tea, I notice her hands are steadier than mine have been all day. Whatever plan she and the others are working on, it gives her strength. I wish I could feel even a fraction of that certainty.

"Eva," I whisper, glancing toward the door to make sure we're alone. "Do you think... do you think people can change? Become someone completely different from who they started as?"

She pauses in her work, considering the question. Then she shakes her head firmly and points to her heart, then to mine. Whatever changes I may have been forced to make, she's telling me, my core remains the same.

"But what if I can't remember who that person is anymore?"

This time she moves closer, her gagged face kind but determined. She points to the window, then makes a gesture like something flying away... escaping to freedom. Then she points back to me and nods encouragingly.

She believes I'm still in here somewhere, the person I was before Gaspard broke me down and rebuilt me in his preferred image. The question is whether that person is strong enough to survive what's coming.

A knock at the door interrupts my thoughts. "Come in."

Gaspard enters, already dressed in his dinner jacket, looking every inch the successful politician and devoted husband. His gaze sweeps over the dress Eva has selected and he nods approvingly.

"Excellent choice. The Fontaines will be impressed." He checks his watch. "We leave in a half hour. I trust you'll be ready?"

"Yes, Sir."

"Good." He steps closer, his hand coming up to adjust the collar at my throat. "Remember what we discussed this morning. The Fontaines are important donors, and Mrs. Fontaine has been vocal about her admiration for our... unconventional love story. I want her to see how happy we are."

Happy. The word sits like poison in my mouth.

"I understand."

"Do you? Because your recent behavior suggests otherwise." His fingers tighten slightly on the collar. "I need my real wife tonight, *ma souris.* Not this hollow version you've been presenting."

"I'll do better."

"See that you do." He releases the collar and steps back. "Eva, finish helping her get ready. And wife? Smile. You're supposed to be in love, remember?"

After he leaves, I sink into the chair at my vanity, staring at my reflection. The woman looking back at me is a stranger—pale, thin, with eyes that hold too much knowledge of pain. How am I supposed to convince anyone that this face belongs to a happily married woman?

Eva moves behind me and begins working on my hair, her touch gentle and soothing. In the mirror, I watch her hands as she styles the dark strands into an elegant updo. For a moment, I let myself imagine what it would be like to have this be normal—getting ready for a pleasant dinner with friends, choosing jewelry because I like it rather than because it sends the right message.

But that's not my life. My life is performance, survival, and the desperate hope that rescue will come before I lose myself completely in the role I'm forced to play.

"Mmph," Eva's muffled voice says through the gag as she steps back to admire her work.

I look like the perfect political wife now, sitting there polished, elegant, and completely put together. The collar glints at my throat like expensive jewelry rather than the chain it truly is.

"Thank you," I whisper, meeting her eyes in the mirror. "For everything."

She places a hand on my shoulder and squeezes gently. Then she gathers her things and heads for the door, pausing only to look back at me with an expression that clearly says: be strong.

Alone again, I practice smiling in the mirror. The first few attempts look more like grimaces, but gradually I manage something that might pass for contentment in dim lighting.

I can do this. I've been doing it for months. One more dinner, one more performance, one more night of pretending to be someone I'm not.

And maybe, if I'm very lucky, it will be one of the last times I have to.

17

MADDIE

I MUST'VE DONE SOMETHING RIGHT BECAUSE when we get home from the dinner, Gaspard tells me I can spend *two* hours with Emilie in the nursery.

"You were perfect tonight, *ma souris*," he says, his hand resting possessively on my lower back as we climb the stairs. "Charming, engaged, everything a political wife should be. Mrs. Fontaine was particularly taken with you."

"Thank you, Sir." The words come automatically, but inside I'm already focused on the gift he's given me... an extra hour with my daughter.

"I'm pleased you've remembered how to be the woman I fell in love with," he continues. "This is who you are when you're not fighting against what's best for you."

I nod, not trusting myself to speak. Let him think his training is working. Let him believe I've accepted my place. As long as it means more time with Emilie, I'll play whatever role he wants.

When we reach the nursery, the nurse who gave me the message looks up from where she's preparing Emilie's nighttime bottle. Her eyes widen slightly at seeing both of us—usually Gaspard doesn't accompany me for these visits.

"Mr. Malveaux," she says, standing quickly. "I wasn't expecting—"

"My wife has earned some extra time with our daughter tonight," he announces, his chest puffing with pride as if my performance was somehow his accomplishment. "Two hours instead of one. She's been an exemplary wife today."

Her gaze flicks to me, and I see understanding there. She knows how carefully I have to navigate his moods.

"Of course. Emilie just finished her bottle, so she should be alert and happy."

Gaspard moves to the crib where Emilie lies on her back, her little arms waving in the air. At four and a half months, she's become so much more aware of her surroundings, her dark eyes tracking movement and her mouth forming shapes that almost look like attempts at words.

"Look at her," he says, but his tone is different

from when he talks about me or our future. Clinical. Assessing. "She's developing well, but she's still so... small. Fragile."

Something in his voice makes my stomach tighten. "She's perfect for her age I think..."

"Perfect, yes, but..." He trails off, watching as Emilie kicks her legs and makes soft cooing sounds. "Well, no matter. You have your time together."

He kisses my forehead—a gesture that would look loving to anyone watching but feels like marking territory to me—and leaves us alone.

I immediately go to the crib, my heart swelling as Emilie's face lights up when she sees me. Her whole body seems to wiggle with excitement, and she reaches up with those tiny hands as if she knows exactly who I am.

"Hello, my beautiful girl," I whisper, lifting her into my arms. She's heavier than last week, more solid, and when she snuggles against my chest, I feel that familiar fierce rush of love that makes everything else fade away.

The nurse busies herself with tidying the already immaculate nursery, giving us privacy while staying close enough to supervise. As I settle into the rocking chair with Emilie, she leans in close.

"Your friend sends word," she murmurs so

quietly I barely catch it. "Plans are progressing. Be ready."

My heart leaps, but I keep my expression neutral. I don't care how she's getting these messages, I'm thrilled either way even if I can't show it. "How long?"

"Soon. Maybe two weeks."

Two weeks. I can survive two more weeks. I press a kiss to Emilie's soft hair, breathing in that sweet baby scent that always calms me.

"Did you hear that, sweetheart?" I whisper almost inaudibly against her head. "Mama's going to take you somewhere safe very soon."

Emilie responds with a happy gurgle, her tiny hand wrapping around my finger with surprising strength. She's grown so much in the couple weeks —her hair is thicker, her eyes more alert, and she's started making sounds that almost resemble laughter when something delights her.

"She's really thriving," she observes, her voice carrying genuine warmth. "Her motor skills are advanced for her age. See how she tracks your face? That's excellent development."

As if to prove the point, Emilie turns her head toward the nurse's voice, then back to me, her expression serious as if she's studying both of us.

"She's so smart," I breathe. "Sometimes I think she understands more than she should at her age."

"Babies are more perceptive than people give them credit for," she says. "They pick up on emotions, on tension in their environment. It's remarkable how adaptable they are."

The words carry a weight beyond their surface meaning. Emilie has been living in this house of shadows and secrets her entire short life, yet she's still developing beautifully. She's resilient, just like her mother has had to be.

For the next hour and a half, I treasure every moment. I rock her, sing softly to her, play simple games that make her eyes widen with delight. When she gets fussy, I know exactly how to comfort her, and when she's content, her trust in me is absolute.

"You're such a good mother," the nurse says as my time begins to wind down. "She knows how much you love her."

"I'd do anything for her," I reply, and mean it with every fiber of my being. "Anything to keep her safe."

"I know you would."

As the two hours come to an end, I hold Emilie a little tighter, memorizing the feel of her warm weight against my chest, the soft sound of her breathing, the way her tiny fingers curl around mine.

"I love you so much, Emilie," I whisper. "More

than you'll ever know. And soon we're going to have a real life together. A safe life."

When I finally have to put her back in the crib, she looks up at me with those serious eyes, and I swear she's trying to tell me something. That she understands. That she'll wait for me.

"Goodnight, my sweet baby," I breathe, stroking her cheek one last time.

As I leave the nursery, my heart is fuller than it's been in weeks. Two extra hours, the promise of rescue in two weeks, and the knowledge that my daughter is healthy and strong.

For the first time in months, the future looks bright.

If only I knew how quickly that brightness could be extinguished.

ANOTHER WEEK PASSES IN CAREFUL performance. The campaign rally goes smoothly—I smile at the right moments, nod approvingly during Gaspard's speech about family values, and play the role of the devoted wife so convincingly that several women in the crowd tell me afterward how lucky I am.

It makes me sick. *Lucky.* If they only knew.

The drive home is filled with Gaspard's pleased commentary on my behavior.

"You were flawless tonight, *ma souris*," he says, his hand resting on my knee as the car winds through the city streets. "Absolutely radiant. The way you connected with one constituent about her grandchildren—wonderful."

"Thank you, Sir."

"You've been so good lately. So... compliant. It's exactly what I hoped marriage would do for you." His fingers squeeze my knee. "You're finally understanding your place in this family, in my life."

I keep my expression serene, even as his praise makes my skin crawl. "I'm trying to be the wife you deserve."

"And you're succeeding beautifully." He leans back in his seat, satisfaction radiating from him. "But remember, *ma souris*, perfection must be maintained. One slip, one moment of defiance, one hint of the rebellious girl you used to be, and you'll remember why complete obedience is necessary. Are we understood?"

My stomach tightens at the threat, but I nod. "Yes, Sir. Completely."

"Good. Because I have such wonderful plans for our future, and I need you to be the perfect partner in all of them."

The rest of the ride passes in comfortable

silence—at least, comfortable for him. I spend the time thinking about my precious hour with Emilie waiting for me at home. It's become the highlight of my days, the reward that makes all the performance and submission bearable.

Back at the house, dinner is served right on time. Gaspard is in an expansive mood, talking about the positive response to tonight's event and his rising poll numbers. I listen and respond at appropriate moments, but mostly I'm calculating how much time until I can see Emilie.

"The Bernards have invited us to their anniversary party next month," he says over dessert. "It will be an excellent opportunity for you to strengthen those social connections."

"Of course. I'd be honored to attend."

"Perfect. See how easy things are when you embrace your role instead of fighting it?"

After we finish eating, I wait for his usual dismissal—the casual wave that means I can go spend my hour in the nursery. Instead, he remains seated when I stand once the plates have been taken, studying me with those calculating eyes.

"Sir?"

"Sit down, Madeline. There's something we need to discuss."

My heart starts to race, but I sink back into my chair, folding my hands in my lap. "Of course."

"You've been asking about Emilie more frequently lately. Mentioning her during our conversations, inquiring about her development."

"I... I'm her mother. It's natural to be concerned about her welfare."

"Natural, yes. But also potentially... distracting." He swirls the wine in his glass, not meeting my eyes. "A woman in your position needs to focus on the future, not remain overly attached to past complications."

Past complications. The phrase makes my blood turn to ice.

"I don't understand, Sir."

"I think you do." Now he looks at me directly, and something in his expression makes the room feel suddenly cold. "Emilie has been... relocated. To a family better equipped to give her the attention she deserves."

The words hit me like physical blows. For a moment, I can't process what he's saying.

"Relocated?" My voice sounds strange, distant.

"She's no longer in this house, wife. The arrangement has been finalized."

The dining room suddenly feels like it's tilting. I grip the edge of the table, trying to anchor myself to reality.

"What do you mean, arrangement?"

"I mean she's gone. And before you become

hysterical, understand that this was always the plan. A child conceived from before we married was never going to be a permanent part of our family dynamic."

Gone.

Emilie is gone.

My baby, my daughter, the one perfect thing in my life—gone.

Something inside me simply stops working. The part of me that feels, that processes emotion, that reacts to devastating news. It just... shuts down.

I sit there, staring at Gaspard's face as he continues explaining his reasoning, but I can't hear the words anymore. There's a ringing in my ears, a numbness spreading through my body like anesthesia.

Emilie is gone.

And I go completely, utterly numb.

18

ANTOSHA

THE CAFÉ FEELS DIFFERENT THIS TIME WHEN Claire arrives—her usual composed demeanor is gone, replaced by something that looks like barely contained panic. She slides into the seat across from me and Guillame without her customary greeting, her hands shaking as she reaches for the coffee cup I've ordered for her.

"What's happened?" I ask immediately, my stomach already dropping at her expression.

"I've been dismissed," she says without preamble. "This morning. No explanation, told by a random guard that my services were no longer required."

Guillame leans forward. "Why? Did Malveaux suspect something?"

"I don't think so. It's because..." Her voice breaks slightly. "The baby... Emilie... she's gone."

The words hit me like a physical blow. "What do you mean, gone?"

"They took her while Malveaux and Maddie were at that campaign rally two nights ago." Claire's hands tremble around her coffee cup. "Then I was dismissed when I arrived this morning. Said my services were no longer needed since there was no child to care for."

My hands clench into fists on the table. "Took her where?"

"I don't know. All I heard was him telling security it was a 'private arrangement' and that no one was to discuss it. But the timing..." She shakes her head. "He planned it deliberately. Made sure Madeline wasn't there when it happened."

"How did Madeline react when she found out?" Guillame's voice is carefully controlled, but I can see the fury building in his eyes.

"I don't know. I was dismissed before I could see her reaction. But Eva managed to get word to me through Marcus—one of the guards—that Madeline hasn't left her bedroom except for meals. She's been confined to just three areas now: the library, the back patio under heavy guard, and the bedroom."

I push back from the table, needing to move, to do something with the rage coursing through me. "He's isolating her completely."

"It gets worse. Marcus said security has been tripled. New protocols, more guards, electronic locks on doors that were never locked before. It's like he's expecting someone to try something."

"Or he's making sure she can't try something herself," Guillame mutters grimly.

Claire nods. "Eva's hasn't been able to communicate with her in forever, is barely allowed to see her. Everything is monitored, controlled. And with me gone..." She looks directly at me. "She has no allies left."

The coffee cup shatters in my grip, the ceramic cutting into my palm as hot liquid spreads across the table. I don't even feel the pain.

"We move now," I say flatly.

"Antosha—"

"No. I'm not leaving her in there another day. Not after what he's done."

Guillame pulls napkins from the dispenser, pressing them against my bleeding hand. "And how exactly do you propose we get through tripled security and electronic locks?"

"Emergency services," Claire says quietly. "Something he can't control or stop, even with all his power."

We both look at her. "What do you mean?"

"Fire department, ambulance, police—when there's a real emergency, they have legal authority to enter any property. Malveaux's influence wouldn't matter if there was a legitimate crisis requiring immediate response."

"What kind of crisis?" Guillame asks, his expression shifting to one of interest.

"I'm not sure but we can think of something." Claire's voice grows stronger as she speaks. "Something that would require immediate evacuation and emergency response. The kind of situation where security protocols become secondary to public safety."

I lean forward despite the throbbing in my hand. "Could you arrange something like that?"

"I still have contacts at the hospital, people in emergency services who owe me favors. If multiple emergency calls came in reporting the same crisis..." She nods slowly. "Yes, I think I could arrange it."

"The timing would have to be perfect," Guillame warns. "And we'd need to know exactly where Madeline is when it happens."

"That would probably be impossible to know with no word from inside now."

"Then what do we do?" I ask, feeling hopeless despite the tentative plan. "We can't risk her getting harmed."

Claire's expression hardens. "Then we create an emergency so big that it doesn't matter where she is—they'll have to evacuate the entire house."

For the first time in days, I feel something other than helpless rage. This could work. It's dangerous, reckless, and a dozen things could go wrong. But it's better than leaving Maddie to suffer while we make perfect plans.

"How long do you need?" I ask.

"Two days to coordinate with my contacts. Three at most."

"Do it," I say. "Whatever it takes."

Claire stands to leave, gathering her purse with hands that are steadier now that we have a plan. "That little girl didn't deserve what happened to her. Neither does her mother."

She pauses at the edge of our table. "There's one more thing. Eva managed to get word out that Maddie hasn't been eating. Barely sleeping. She's... breaking down. Whatever we're going to do, we need to do it soon."

After she's gone, Guillame and I sit in silence for several minutes, both lost in our own thoughts.

"This is going to be messy," he finally says.

"I know."

"And if it goes wrong, Madeline could be hurt in the chaos."

"She's already being hurt. At least this way, she has a chance."

He nods slowly. "Then let's go save your girl."

As we leave the café and head home to begin preparations, I think about Madeline sitting in that house, isolated and grieving. Two or three more days of hell, and then—God willing—we get her out.

The only question is whether there will be enough left of her to save.

THE DAYS WAITING HAVE BEEN UNBEARABLE. I can't sit, can't think, can't stop pacing. Every time I close my eyes, I see her — locked behind those electronic doors, fading piece by piece while Malveaux tightens his hold. The thought gnaws at me, relentless, a constant reminder that every second she remains there, she becomes smaller, quieter, and more fragile.

Uncle told me to conserve my strength, to think logically until Claire sets the plan in motion. Easy for him. He doesn't wake in the middle of the night tasting her kiss, feeling her warmth linger on his skin as if it were a brand, a promise, a warning.

I press my palms into the edge of the desk until my bandaged hand throbs, trying to ground myself in pain instead of memory. But it doesn't work. Because the memory comes anyway, unbidden, as if my body wants to torture me.

That day at the beach—her pink blouse, the way she had giggled at the idea of a surprise, how her eyes widened when the car pulled up to the private shore. She had squealed, slung her arms around my neck, pure impulse, pure joy. The sound of it echoes in my head now, soft and insistent, taunting me with its innocence. And then, in the water... fuck! She had looked at me as if I were the only safe thing in her world.

I should have walked away. Should have left her to play in the waves alone. But she came to me, lips parted with a question she shouldn't have asked, eyes on my mouth, hands on my chest. And when she kissed me...

I shut my eyes, dragging in a rough breath. The memory burns hotter than any fire Claire could conjure to get us inside that house. Because that kiss wasn't duty, wasn't protection, wasn't survival. It was choice. Hers.

That's what Malveaux will never understand, what he can never force. Affection given freely from Maddie; her smile, her laugh, her lips. He can trap her, starve her, drug her, break her down, but he can't take that from her. And God help me, I can't lose it either. Not after she chose to give me that moment.

I shove away from the desk, heart pounding

hard enough to shake my ribs. The wait is almost over.

Until then, all I can do is remember the taste of saltwater on her lips and cling to the vow I made in the waves: she won't drown. Not while I'm here.

The phone rings, cutting through my spiraling thoughts. I grab it before the second ring.

"Antosha?" Claire's voice is tight with urgency. "We need to change plans."

My blood turns to ice. "Why?"

"Malveaux has dismissed Eva, too, as of this morning, Madeline has no contact with anyone except him. No meals with staff, no supervised visits to the library or patio. She's completely isolated now."

The room spins around me. "Fuck. What for?"

"We don't know. But Marcus thinks something spooked him. Maybe he suspects someone's been communicating with the outside, or maybe..." Her voice trails off.

"Maybe what?"

"Maybe he's preparing for something. Marcus heard him on a phone call talking about 'new beginnings' and 'clearing away complications.'"

New beginnings. The phrase makes my skin crawl because I know exactly what it means coming from a man like Malveaux. He's going to start over with Madeline, rebuild her from scratch now that he's removed every trace of comfort or hope from her life.

"How long until you can trigger the emergency?" I ask, forcing my voice to remain steady.

"Tonight. I've coordinated with my contacts—gas leak reports will start coming in around in a couple hours, multiple sources claiming they smell gas near the property. Fire department will have to respond, and once they're there..."

"They'll have to search the entire house for the source."

"Exactly. But Antosha, with no inside help, with no way to know where she is or what condition she's in..." Claire's voice grows worried. "This is going to be chaos. Pure chaos."

"Good," I say grimly. "Chaos is exactly what we need."

Because in chaos, even the most carefully laid plans can crumble. And maybe, in all that confusion, we'll finally get our chance to bring Madeline home.

I hang up the phone and sink into my chair, staring out the window at the gathering dusk. After months of watching her suffer from a distance, months of feeling helpless while that monster destroys everything good about her, we finally act.

One way or another, tonight everything will change.

I close my eyes and make the same promise I've been making for weeks: Hold on, *ma petite*. Just hold on a little longer.

19

MADDIE

THE DAYS SINCE GASPARD CRUELLY announced he gave my baby away have bled one into another. Every day is the same, with all the small joy I had left stripped away. My life is hollow, like my heart, and I no longer feel like fighting.

I thought Gaspard couldn't get to me, not truly. But he knew. Somehow, he knew that taking away my daughter would break me completely.

And he was right.

I move through each day like a ghost, performing my duties with mechanical precision. I smile when he expects me to smile. I nod when he speaks. I wear the dresses he chooses and sit where he tells me to sit. I've become the perfect wife he always wanted—compliant, beautiful, empty yet performative.

"You look lovely this morning, *ma souris*," he

says over breakfast, his tone pleased as he takes in my appearance. My hair is styled in an elegant chignon, my makeup flawless despite the fact that I can barely remember applying it myself without Eva's help.

"Thank you, Sir." The words come automatically, without thought or feeling.

"I have some wonderful news to share with you this morning," he continues, cutting his eggs with precise movements. "I've made some important decisions about our household arrangements."

I nod because it's expected. "Of course."

"Eva will be leaving us today. With no child to care for and you being such a perfect wife now, her services are no longer required."

The words hit me like a physical blow, but I force my expression to remain neutral. Eva. My last connection to anything resembling kindness in this house.

"I see," I manage.

"It's for the best, really. You and I need to focus entirely on each other, on our future together." His hand reaches across the space between us to cover mine. "And speaking of your safety and our future —from now on, you'll be with me at all times. Everywhere I go, you'll accompany me. Every meeting, every appointment, every moment of my day."

My throat tightens. "Even..."

"Even to use the bathroom, yes. I won't have my wife out of my sight for even a moment. It's the only way I can ensure your complete safety, and the safety of any children we might be blessed with." His thumb strokes across my knuckles possessively. "You understand, don't you? How precious you are to me?"

Precious. Like a valuable object to be guarded.

"Yes, Sir. I understand."

"Good. This way, I can protect you from any... outside influences that might try to interfere with our happiness." His smile is warm but his eyes are calculating. "Complete togetherness, complete safety. Isn't that what every married couple dreams of?"

I nod because it's what he expects, even as the last shred of hope dies inside me. No Eva. No moments alone. No possibility of help or rescue or even a minute to think clearly.

Complete isolation disguised as devotion.

After breakfast, Eva appears in the doorway to say goodbye. For the first time in as long as I can remember, she's not gagged—perhaps Gaspard's final cruelty, allowing me to hear her voice one last time before losing her forever.

"Goodbye, Madame," she says quietly, her eyes bright with unshed tears. "Take care of yourself."

"Thank you, Eva. For everything."

She nods once, then turns and walks away, leaving me more alone than I've ever been in my life.

The rest of the morning passes in a blur. Gaspard takes me to his first meeting, where I sit silently in a corner while he discusses municipal contracts. Then to lunch with potential donors, where I smile and nod and play the devoted wife. Every bathroom break requires his escort, every moment monitored and controlled.

"You're doing beautifully," he murmurs in my ear as we return home in the afternoon. "This is exactly what I envisioned for us."

His study is warm, a fire crackling in the large stone fireplace. His desk is positioned to catch the natural light from the tall windows, papers and files neatly organized across its surface.

"Kneel by the fire," he instructs, settling into his chair behind the desk. "The light will be better there if I need you to review anything."

I move to the fireplace as directed, sinking to my knees on the thick Persian rug. The warmth from the flames feels good against my skin, though I register it distantly, as if experiencing it through a heavy fog.

"Perfect," he murmurs, already turning his

attention to his paperwork. "Such a lovely picture you make."

He begins making phone calls, his voice shifting into the authoritative tone he uses for business. I kneel in place, my hands folded in my lap, staring into the dancing flames. The fire tools hang on their stand beside me—poker, shovel, brush, tongs—all neatly arranged and gleaming in the firelight.

Time passes. An hour, maybe more. Gaspard's voice drones on as he discusses polling numbers and campaign strategies, the sound becoming mere background noise to my empty thoughts.

Then the poker catches my eye.

It's wrought iron, heavy and solid, with an ornate handle that speaks of craftsmanship and expense. A tool meant for tending fires, for moving logs and coals. But as I stare at it, my numb mind begins to focus for the first time in days.

A weapon.

The thought comes unbidden, cutting through the fog that has surrounded me since learning of Emilie's fate. For the first time since that terrible dinner, I feel something other than emptiness. Something hot and fierce and dangerous.

Rage.

He took my daughter. My baby. The one perfect, innocent thing in my life, and he gave her away like she was nothing. Like she was a problem to be solved rather than a child to be loved.

And now Eva. Gone. My last friend, my only ally, dismissed because my isolation wasn't complete enough for his liking.

My hands clench in my lap as the fury builds, burning away the numbness that has protected me these past days. Every injustice, every cruelty, every moment of degradation comes flooding back with crystal clarity.

The collar around my neck. The bruises hidden beneath my clothes. The forced smiles and empty words. The nights of violation disguised as marriage. The complete control over every aspect of my existence.

And now this—never to be alone again, never to have even a moment's privacy, monitored and guarded like a prisoner who can't be trusted with five minutes of solitude.

Gaspard continues his phone conversation, oblivious to the change taking place mere feet away. He's discussing voter demographics, his tone confident and pleased with himself.

I look at the poker again.

Then I look at him.

And for the first time in months, I make a choice that has nothing to do with survival or submission or playing a role.

I choose violence.

Moving slowly, quietly, I reach for the poker. Its weight is substantial in my hands, the metal still warm from the fire. Gaspard doesn't notice as I rise to my feet, the weapon held behind my back.

He's still on the phone, turned completely away from me in his chair as he references something in his files. Completely unaware that his perfect, broken wife is no longer kneeling on the floor in submission, but about take back her life.

I take a single step toward his desk.

Then another, and another...

"Yes, the polling data looks excellent," he's saying. "We should capitalize on it." A pause, then "Terrific. Let me know."

He catches sight of my shadow right as he hangs up the call and turns while beginning to stand, but it is too fucking late as I swing the poker right at his head.

The poker connects with a thud that echoes through the silent room... a hymn of rebellion. It hits with a force that I feel from my wrists to my shoulder, and he stumbles down, a dance of shock and pain.

His fall doesn't silence him; he spits curses, clawing his way up like a vengeful spirit. But I've tasted power, the bitter tang of justice, and can't let it slip away.

Over and over, I swing the poker as he lifts his hands to try and protect himself, a chorus of grunts and metallic rings tattooing the air. Each strike a word unsaid, a scream for Emilie, for everything he's stolen.

Blood—anointing the poker, my hands, and the floor—marks a line I've crossed from which I can't return. My arms ache, the poker a leaden extension of my fragmented soul. But there's no stopping until, through the haze of red, there he is. On the floor, quiet and silent and for once, I'm the one towering over him wielding all the power.

He's bleeding, his head and face covered in wounds, and I drop the poker at the horrifying sight of what I've done.

I'm trembling, my breaths coming in ragged gasps, as I stare at Gaspard's lifeless body. The sight of him, bloodied and broken, should fill me with fear, but all I feel is a sense of relief. He can't hurt me or anyone else anymore.

But I can't stay here. I need to get as far away from this place as possible.

With a newfound sense of urgency, I search Gaspard's desk for any information on Emilie, but there's nothing. Then, I spot a gun in the drawer. My fingers brush against the cold metal, and I wrap my hand around it, feeling its weight and power. I've never used a gun before, but I'm willing to do whatever it takes to get the hell out of here.

I take a deep breath, steeling myself for what's to come, and exit the office. The hallways are quiet, but it won't be long before someone discovers Gaspard's body and raises the alarm. I need to be gone by then.

I make my way through the house, my heart pounding in my chest, aching for my daughter. I don't know who Gaspard gave her away to, but I'm determined to find her once I'm away from this house of horror.

As I round a corner, I nearly run into one of Gaspard's guards. He's a tall, imposing man, with a cold, hard look in his eyes. I see the surprise in his face as he takes in the sight of me, holding a gun and covered in blood.

But I don't hesitate. I raise the gun, my hand steady and sure, and point it at him. "I'll kill you," I say, my voice low and dangerous. "Just like I killed him."

The guard's eyes widen, and he steps back, raising his hands in surrender. There is fear in his face, and it gives me a sense of satisfaction. I'm not the helpless, frightened girl I once was. And even though this man has probably been trapped as much as I have, there's no forgiveness from me for everyone here allowing Gaspard's treatment of me.

But I don't want to kill anyone else.

I only want two things—my freedom and to find out where my baby is and get her back.

Walking cautiously past the guard, I keep the gun pointed at him to avoid any attempt to tackle me, and continue through the house—luckily, with no one else trying to stop me—until finally, I see the front door. The cool night air hits my face as I push it open, heart racing with excitement and fear.

And that's when I see all the emergency vehicles rushing down the driveway toward the house.

20

MADDIE

THE FLASHING LIGHTS ARE BLINDING AGAINST the darkness—red, blue, white strobes cutting through the night like angry stars. Fire trucks, ambulances, police cars, all screaming toward the house with sirens wailing.

I stand frozen in the doorway, the gun still clutched in my bloodied hand, watching as what looks like half the city's emergency services converges on Gaspard's estate. The cool night air hits my face, sharp and clean after the suffocating atmosphere inside, but I can barely register it over the chaos unfolding before me.

What is this? What's happening?

The first responders are already jumping from their vehicles, shouting orders about gas leaks and evacuation protocols. Men in hazmat suits are rushing toward the house, their equipment catching the light from the emergency vehicles.

"Ma'am!" A paramedic spots me in the doorway and starts running toward me. "Ma'am, you need to get away from the building immediately! There's been a gas leak reported—the whole structure could be compromised!"

Gas leak? There's no gas leak. But I don't correct him. Instead, I let him guide me away from the house, the gun hidden behind my back as we move toward the cluster of emergency vehicles.

"Are you injured?" he asks, his flashlight beam catching the blood on my clothes. "Ma'am, you're covered in blood—"

"It's not mine," I say quietly. The words feel strange on my tongue, but they're true. The blood painting my dress, my hands, my arms—none of it belongs to me.

"Okay, let's get you checked out anyway. Were you alone in the house?"

Before I can answer, more shouts erupt from the emergency teams. Someone's found the guard I passed in the hallway, and he's telling them about Gaspard's body in the study. About me.

About what I've done.

Panic flares in my chest, but before I can run, before I can even think clearly about what to do next, I see two familiar figures pushing through the crowd of first responders.

Guillame. And beside him, looking desperate and determined...

Antosha.

Our eyes meet across the chaos, and for a moment, everything else fades away. The sirens, the shouting, the blood on my clothes—none of it matters because he's here. After all these months of captivity, all these weeks of being completely isolated, Antosha is here.

"Maddie!" He breaks away from his uncle, pushing past emergency workers to reach me.

The paramedic tries to stop him. "Sir, this is a crime scene—"

"She's my family," Antosha says firmly, his voice carrying enough authority that the man hesitates.

Then Antosha's arms are around me, and I'm sobbing against his chest; great, heaving sobs that feel like they're tearing me apart from the inside. The gun slips from my nerveless fingers, clattering to the pavement.

"It's okay," he murmurs into my hair. "You're safe now. I'm here."

But I'm not safe. I'm a murderer. And any moment now, the police are going to figure out what I've done and arrest me.

"Antosha," I gasp against his chest. "I killed him. I killed Gaspard."

"Shh." His arms tighten around me. "Stop talking. We're going to handle this."

"No, you don't understand—" I pull back to look at him, needing him to see the truth in my eyes. "I beat him with a poker. There was so much blood, and he was lying there, and I—"

"Maddie." Guillame appears beside us, his expression grim but not shocked. "No more. We need to get you away from here. Now."

"She needs medical attention," the paramedic protests. "And the police will want to question her about—"

"About what?" Guillame's voice carries the kind of quiet authority that comes from years of wielding power. "About being a victim of domestic abuse who was trapped in a house with a gas leak? She's clearly in shock."

The paramedic looks uncertain, glancing between us and the chaos surrounding the house. More emergency workers are streaming in and out, some carrying equipment, others coordinating the evacuation. In all the confusion, it's hard to focus on any one thing.

"The guard inside said there was a body," another officer says, approaching our group. "Someone needs to—"

"Body?" Guillame raises an eyebrow. "In a house with a potentially explosive gas leak? Are you certain that's wise?"

The officer looks frustrated. "Sir, we have protocols—"

"And I have lawyers," Guillame replies smoothly. "This woman is clearly a victim who needs immediate medical care. Everything else can wait until the building is declared safe."

I watch this exchange with growing amazement. Somehow, in the midst of all this chaos, Guillame is managing to redirect attention away from what I've done. The emergency about the gas leak, fake though it must be, is providing cover for my escape.

"Come on," Antosha says softly, his arm still around me. "Let's get you out of here."

But as we start to move toward one of the cars, I hear shouting from inside the house. Someone's found Gaspard. Someone's calling for detectives.

The paramedic who was treating me turns toward the commotion, then back to us, his expression changing as he pieces things together.

"Wait," he calls out. "The woman! She said the blood wasn't hers. If someone's bleeding inside—"

That's when I know it's over. The brief moment of hope, of thinking I might actually escape the consequences of what I've done, crumbles as reality crashes back down.

Police officers are already moving in our direction, their expressions shifting from concerned to suspicious as they take in my blood-covered appearance and the growing commotion from inside the house.

"Ma'am," one of them says, his hand moving to rest on his service weapon. "I need you to step away from these gentlemen and put your hands where I can see them."

Antosha's arm tightens around me protectively. "She's a victim—"

"Sir, step back. Now."

I look up at Antosha, memorizing his face in the flashing lights of the emergency vehicles. After months of dreaming about this moment, about him coming to rescue me, it's ending before it even begins.

If only I had waited a little longer... but it's too late now.

"I'm sorry," I whisper to him. "I'm so sorry."

Then I step out of his arms and raise my hands, the blood on them visible to everyone as the officer approaches with handcuffs.

"You have the right to remain silent," he begins, but his words fade into background noise as I watch Antosha's face twist with anguish.

I'm finally free from Gaspard.

But I'll never be truly free again.

THE COUNTY JAIL'S MEDICAL FACILITY IS sterile and cold, nothing like the luxury I've become accustomed to over the past months. But after the suffocating opulence of Gaspard's house, the bare walls and harsh fluorescent lighting feel almost honest.

"We need to document everything for evidence," the nurse explains as she photographs the blood splatter on my arms and dress. "Standard procedure in cases like this."

Cases like this. Murder cases.

I sit on the examination table in the paper gown they've given me, my bloodstained clothes now sealed in evidence bags. Somehow they also managed to remove the choker and strangely, I miss the weight of it. My neck feels... exposed.

The reality of what I've done, what's going to happen to me, keeps hitting in waves. One moment I feel numb, disconnected from it all. The next, panic threatens to overwhelm me completely.

"Blood pressure's elevated," the nurse murmurs, making notes on her clipboard. "Pulse rapid. When did you last eat?"

I have to think about it. Time has become fluid since I brought that poker down on Gaspard's head. "This afternoon, I think. Maybe this morning."

"We'll get you something after we finish here." She moves to a cabinet, retrieving several vials and a needle. "I need to draw blood for testing. Standard procedure."

I don't ask what they're testing for. DNA evidence, probably. Proof that I was there, that I did what they already know I did. The needle barely registers—such a small pain compared to everything else.

"Any chance you could be pregnant?" she asks as she labels the vials.

The question hits me like a physical blow. With everything that's happened, I hadn't even thought... But it's been over a month since that night when Gaspard used the ovulation test, when he was so determined to get me pregnant again.

"I... I don't know. Maybe."

She nods, making another note. "We'll include that in the blood work then. Results should be back in a few hours."

Hours pass in a blur of procedures and questions. Fingerprints. Photographs. A brief consultation with a public defender who looks barely old enough to drive, let alone handle a murder case. Through it all, I keep thinking about Antosha's face in those emergency lights, the way he looked when they put the handcuffs on me.

I don't know if I'll ever see him again.

The nurse returns as evening settles over the jail after I've eaten dinner, her expression neutral but not unkind.

"Your blood work came back," she says, settling into the chair across from my narrow cot.

I brace myself for whatever evidence they've found, whatever proof will seal my fate.

"You are pregnant, ma'am."

Of course. Gaspard made sure to time everything perfectly, down to the ovulation test. I'm not surprised at all that there's another baby, one that was growing inside me even as I was beating their father to death.

"Are you okay?" the nurse asks, studying my face with professional concern.

Am I okay? I'm a pregnant woman in jail for murder. The father of my unborn child is dead by my own hand. My first child has been given away to strangers. The man I love watched me get arrested and may never see me again.

But for the first time in months, I'm not living under Gaspard's roof. I'm not wearing his collar or playing his perfect wife or enduring his touch. He can never hurt me again, can never take another child from me, can never destroy anyone else the way he destroyed me.

"I don't know," I say honestly.

The nurse nods as if she understands. "Given your situation, there are options we should discuss. Programs for pregnant inmates, medical care, counseling services."

Options. As if I have any real choices left.

But as I place my hand over my still-flat stomach, I realize I do have one choice. Maybe the only one that truly matters.

This baby, one conceived in violence and control, doesn't have to be defined by those circumstances. I couldn't save Emilie from him, couldn't protect her from being taken away. But this child... this one I can keep safe.

Even from prison, I can love them. I can make sure they know they're wanted, that they matter, that they're more than the sum of their father's sins.

"What happens now?" I ask.

"Now you rest. Tomorrow you'll be arraigned, and the legal process will begin. But for tonight, you're safe."

Safe. Such a simple word, but one that's been absent from my vocabulary for so long.

As the nurse leaves and the lights dim for the night, I lie on the narrow cot with my hand still pressed to my stomach. Somewhere out there,

Emilie is with strangers, and I may never see her again. Somewhere out there, Antosha is probably trying to figure out how to help me, though I'm not sure anyone can.

But here, in this moment, it's just me and this new life growing inside me. A child who will never know their father's cruelty, who will never have to endure what I endured.

I close my eyes and whisper the first promise I've been able to make in months. "I'll protect you. Whatever happens to me, I'll make sure you're safe."

For the first time since that terrible night when Gaspard told me Emilie was gone, I allow myself to hope.

Even if it's from behind bars, even if everything else is uncertain, I'm going to be a mother again.

And that hope is what I'll hold onto this time, no matter what happens.

21

ANTOSHA

The flashing lights fade into the distance as the police car carrying Madeline disappears down the long driveway, leaving me standing in the chaos of emergency vehicles with the taste of failure bitter in my mouth.

Our rescue plan. Our carefully orchestrated emergency. All of it led to this, watching the woman I love get arrested while covered in her captor's blood.

"We have to follow them," I tell Guillame, already moving toward our car.

"Antosha, wait." His hand on my arm stops me. "Think. Running to the police station right now, demanding to see her. What good will that do?"

"I can't just leave her alone in there."

"She won't be alone. She'll have medical care and people who are trained to handle situations like this." His voice is steady, but I can see the strain around his eyes. "What she needs now is strategy, not emotion."

I want to argue, want to push past him and race after that police car. But he's right. Charging in without a plan will only make things worse.

"We need witnesses," I say suddenly. "People who can testify to what she's been through."

"Eva," Guillame nods immediately. "She was dismissed this morning, but she saw everything. The abuse, isolation, the way Malveaux controlled every aspect of Madeline's life."

"And Marcus, the guard Claire mentioned. If he was sympathetic to helping, maybe he'll be willing to testify."

"If we can find them. And we don't have to worry about NDA's, as they don't cover abuse, but they may fear testifying for other reasons."

"He probably threatened their families or some other bullshit," I say grimly. "We'll have to assure them we'll protect them. Maddie shouldn't have to go to prison for defending herself all because they are afraid."

Before Guillame can respond, one of the fire chiefs approaches us. "You gentlemen need to clear the area. We're still investigating the gas leak."

Gas leak. The fake emergency that brought us

here, that created the chaos that led to... all this bullshit.

"Of course," Guillame replies smoothly. "We were just leaving."

But as we head toward our car, another official intercepts us, a detective with tired eyes and a grim expression.

"I'm Detective Laureaux. I understand you know the woman who was arrested tonight?"

My mouth goes dry. "She's... family."

"I need to inform you that the victim, Gaspard Malveaux, is not deceased. He's in critical condition at the local hospital."

The words hit me like a physical blow. Alive. Malveaux is alive.

Which means Madeline isn't facing murder charges. Not yet, anyway. But it also means that monster might recover, might survive to continue terrorizing her.

"His condition?" Guillame asks.

"Severe head trauma. Significant blood loss. A lot of injuries to his arms from trying to defend himself. The doctors aren't sure if he'll pull through, and if he does..." The detective's expression is carefully neutral. "There may be permanent damage."

Part of me, the part that's watched Madeline suffer from the start, hopes Malveaux never wakes up. But the practical part knows that his survival might actually help her case. Attempted murder carries a lighter sentence than murder, and if she can prove self-defense...

"Will we be able to visit her?" I ask.

"She's being processed now. Won't be available for visitors until tomorrow at the earliest. But she'll have access to legal counsel." The detective studies us both carefully. "You might want to get her a good lawyer. This case is going to be complicated."

AFTER HE LEAVES, GUILLAME AND I DRIVE home in tense silence. The estate feels empty without the possibility of Madeline returning to it, without the hope that's sustained us through weeks of planning.

"The lawyer," I say as we pull into the circular drive. "Call them now."

Guillame nods, already dialing. "Victoria Chen. If anyone can get Madeline out of this, it's her."

While he makes the call, I pace in the study, my mind racing through everything that went wrong tonight. We were so close. If we'd arrived even ten minutes earlier, if we'd been able to get to her before she...

But maybe this was always how it had to end.

Maybe Madeline had to be the one to fight back, to take control of her own fate. I just never imagined it would lead to her trading one prison for another.

"Victoria will meet with her tomorrow morning," Guillame announces, ending his call. "She's already reviewing what she can find about the case."

"What did you tell her?"

"The truth. That Madeline is a victim of long-term domestic abuse who fought back against her captor. That we need to find witnesses who can testify to what she's endured."

"We need to find Eva and Marcus," I remind him immediately. "They likely saw everything."

Guillame nods slowly. "Victoria's team includes investigators. They'll know how to approach people in situations like this, how to offer protection in exchange for testimony. If Malveaux survives, they might worry about retaliation after the fact despite the NDA not being enforceable."

I sink into a chair, suddenly exhausted. "It's my fault. If we hadn't triggered that fake emergency, if we'd waited..."

"She might be dead by now," Guillame says firmly. "Or completely broken beyond repair. What happened tonight? She chose to fight back. That takes strength, Antosha. Strength she might not have had if we'd waited much longer."

Maybe he's right. Maybe our failed rescue attempt gave her the opportunity she needed to save herself, even if it came at a terrible cost.

"The baby," I realize suddenly. "Emilie. Someone needs to find her."

Guillame nods grimly. "Victoria's team will handle that too. Finding the child will be crucial for preparing Madeline's defense; for proving what Malveaux was capable of, what he took from her."

The phone rings, and Guillame answers with a sharp "Yes?"

His expression changes as he listens, growing darker with each passing second.

"What?" I demand when he hangs up.

"That was Victoria. She's already talked to the prosecutor's office." He meets my eyes, his expression grim. "They're going to charge Madeline with attempted murder in the first degree. No bail."

No bail. Which means she'll remain in custody until trial, trapped in another kind of prison while we try to prove she was defending herself.

"How long?"

"Months. Maybe longer if the case goes to trial."

I close my eyes, thinking of Madeline sitting in a jail cell, probably more alone and frightened than she's ever been. After everything she's endured, after finally finding the strength to fight back, she's still not free.

But she's alive. Malveaux can't hurt her anymore, can't touch her or control her or take anything else away from her.

And this time, she won't face it alone. This time, she'll have the best legal defense money can buy, and people who will fight for her freedom with everything we have.

"Tomorrow," I tell Guillame. "We start tomorrow."

"Start what?"

"Building the case that brings her home."

Because I made her a promise months ago, and I intend to keep it. Whatever it takes, however long it takes, I'm going to make sure Madeline gets the happy life she deserves.

Even if I have to tear down the entire system to do it.

THE COUNTY JAIL IS A GRAY, WINDOWLESS block of concrete, more fortress than building. I park in the visitors' lot, my knuckles white on the steering wheel. It takes me too long to shut off the engine, as if keeping it running will keep me from walking through those doors and seeing her behind glass.

But I have to.

Inside, the air smells of disinfectant and metal. The fluorescent lights hum overhead, harsh and unrelenting. I check in with the deputy at the desk, give my name, and wait while he makes a few calls.

"Visiting hours are fifteen minutes," he says flatly. "She'll be behind glass. Keep your conversation appropriate."

Fifteen minutes. After everything she's been through, after everything we've tried to do for her, fifteen minutes is all I get and I can't even hug her. I nod stiffly. "Understood."

They lead me down a corridor lined with cinderblock walls, scuffed with years of use. My pulse hammers with every step.

The deputy opens a heavy metal door, and I step into the visiting area. Rows of booths line the room, each separated by thick glass, telephones hanging on either side. A few are occupied— families, boyfriends, desperate mothers whispering reassurances to frightened sons.

And then I see her.

Madeline sits in one of the booths, her posture stiff, hands folded in her lap. She's wearing the standard orange jumpsuit, her hair pulled back into a rough knot. She looks smaller somehow, but her chin is lifted, her gaze steady. She doesn't look broken, yet I know she must be struggling with everything that's happened.

My throat tightens.

I slide into the seat opposite her, pick up the phone. It takes her a moment to do the same, as if she's weighing whether she can bear to hear my voice.

"Maddie." My voice cracks despite myself. "Are you all right?"

She studies me for a long moment before answering, her voice low and careful. "I've been better."

Her understatement nearly undoes me. I want to reach through the glass, to hold her hand, to tell her none of this was her fault. But the rules of this place are iron, and the deputy at the back of the room watches every move.

"They told me," I say, forcing my voice steady. "No bail. But we've already hired an attorney—Victoria Chen. She's the best. She's meeting with you later today."

Madeline exhales, the tiniest release of breath. Her fingers tighten on the phone. "I don't want you to waste money on me."

"It's not a waste." My jaw clenches. "After everything you've been through, you deserve the best defense anyone can give you. We'll get witnesses, people who saw what Malveaux did to you. We'll prove it was self-defense."

Her gaze flickers, a shadow passing over her features. "He's alive, isn't he?"

"Yes." I pause, watching her expression shift, relief and dread tangled together. "Critical condition. Which means..."

"Which means I'm not a murderer. Yet." Her voice is flat, but I catch the faint tremor at the edge of it.

"You're not a murderer at all," I say fiercely. "You're a survivor. And I swear to you, I'll prove it. Whatever it takes."

She lowers her eyes, fingers curling tightly around the phone. For a moment, silence stretches between us, filled only by the background murmur of other visitors. Then she says, barely above a whisper, "I don't know how to do this, Antosha. I've gone from one cage to another."

The words gut me.

"You won't stay in here forever," I promise. "We'll build a case. We'll bring you home. And Emilie, we'll find her. I don't care how long it takes."

Her eyes lift to mine, shining with a restrained ache. She doesn't cry, won't let herself, but I see it in her—the grief for her child, the weight of everything she's endured, the fragile strength she still somehow carries.

The phone crackles as the deputy calls out, "Five minutes."

I lean closer to the glass, willing her to feel the force of my vow. "Hold on, Maddie. Just hold on a little longer. You're not alone anymore. Not ever again."

Her lips part as if she wants to say something, but the words don't come. Instead, she gives me the smallest nod, her chin trembling.

The deputy calls time, and I have to set the phone down. I press my hand to the glass, a useless gesture, but it's all I have.

She doesn't mirror it. She just watches me, eyes steady, until the guard taps her shoulder and leads her away.

And then she's gone again.

But this time, I swear, I won't fail her.

22

MADDIE

Four months in county jail have taught me that time moves differently when you're waiting for your life to be decided by other people. The days blur together in a haze of gray walls, fluorescent lights, and the constant noise of women who are just as trapped as I am.

But I have something they don't know about, something that's kept me going through the endless procedural hearings and legal delays. Something that makes the nausea I've been hiding behind claims of anxiety worth enduring.

I'm almost twenty weeks pregnant now, and somehow I've managed to keep it secret from everyone except Victoria Chen. The loose-fitting jail uniforms help, and the weight I lost during my final months with Gaspard means the pregnancy weight gain just makes me look healthier rather than obviously expecting.

"Madeline?" The guard's voice cuts through my thoughts as I sit in the common area, pretending to read a book that's been my prop for weeks. "Your lawyer's here."

I follow her down the familiar corridor to the meeting room where Victoria waits, her expensive briefcase and tailored suit a stark contrast to the institutional beige surroundings. She's become my lifeline over these months, the only person fighting for my freedom while I sit helplessly behind bars.

"How are you feeling?" she asks as I settle into the plastic chair across from her. It's become our code since she's one of the few people who knows about the pregnancy, and she worries about the stress affecting the baby.

"Fine. The same." I place my hands on the table, noting how my wedding ring from Gaspard has left a permanent indent on my finger even though they took it away during processing. "Any news?"

Victoria's expression grows grim, and my heart sinks. After four months of waiting, I've learned to read her face, and this isn't the look of someone bearing good news.

"We've hit another dead end with Emilie," she

says softly. "My investigators have traced every lead, followed every paper trail. Whoever Malveaux gave her to, he was very careful to keep their real identities hidden. All the documentation uses false names, shell companies. It's like she just... vanished."

The words hit me like physical blows. Even though I've been preparing myself for this possibility, hearing it confirmed feels like losing her all over again.

"So she's gone," I whisper. "Really gone."

"We're not giving up," Victoria says firmly. "But I wanted to be honest with you about where we stand. Finding her is going to take time we might not have before trial."

I nod, blinking back tears I refuse to shed. Crying won't bring Emilie back, and I need to save my energy for the baby growing inside me - the one person I might actually be able to protect.

"There's something else," Victoria continues, and something in her tone makes me look up sharply. "Malveaux woke up yesterday."

The room seems to tilt around me. "What?"

"He's been conscious for about eighteen hours. The doctors are calling it remarkable; they expected significant brain damage, but his cognitive function appears to be intact. There's scarring, some facial disfigurement from where the poker caught him, but otherwise..." She shrugs. "He's fine."

Fine. The monster who destroyed my life, who stole my daughter, who turned me into this hollow version of myself... he's fine. While I'm sitting in jail for finally defending myself.

Great.

"What does this mean for my case?"

Victoria's expression is carefully neutral, but I can see the concern in her eyes. "He's the only witness to what happened in that office. His testimony will be crucial."

"He'll lie." The words come out flat, matter-of-fact. "He'll say whatever serves him best."

"Maybe. But Madeline, there's something you need to understand. The prosecutor's entire case rests on proving premeditation, that you planned to hurt him. Without physical evidence of immediate threat, without witnesses to ongoing abuse that night..." She leans forward. "His version of events could determine whether you spend the next twenty years in prison or walk free."

Twenty years. The baby inside me would be an adult before I saw freedom again.

"When will he testify?" I ask.

"That's just it; he's requested to see you first. Before he talks to the police, before he gives any official statements. He wants to meet with you privately."

My blood turns to ice. "No."

"Madeline, I know how difficult this would be, but—"

"No." I stand up abruptly, the chair scraping against the floor. "I won't see him. I won't sit in a room with that man and pretend to be grateful that he's alive."

"You might not have a choice." Victoria's voice is gentle but firm. "If he refuses to give a statement without seeing you first, the judge could order it. And frankly, this might be your only chance to influence what he tells the police."

The thought of facing Gaspard again, of sitting across from him and seeing those cold, calculating eyes in his scarred face, makes my stomach churn. But she's right, this could be my only opportunity to secure my freedom.

"He won't help me," I say quietly. "Not unless he gets something in return."

"What could he possibly want from you now?"

I place my hand over my still-hidden belly, thinking about the secret I've kept for four months. About the child growing inside me who shares DNA with the man I tried to kill.

"Everything," I whisper. "He'll want everything."

THREE DAYS LATER, I'M LED INTO A DIFFERENT kind of visiting room, those reserved for private attorney meetings and official business. There's no glass barrier here, just a table and two chairs in a room that smells of stale coffee and fear.

And then he walks in.

Gaspard moves slowly, aided by a cane, but his posture is still commanding. The left side of his face bears a long, jagged scar that runs from his temple to his jaw... a permanent reminder of what I did to him. His left eye is slightly drooped, and when he smiles, it's lopsided.

But his eyes... his eyes are exactly the same. Cold, predatory, calculating.

"Hello, *ma souris*," he says softly as he settles into the chair across from me.

The old endearment makes my skin crawl, but I force myself to meet his gaze. "Gaspard."

"You look well. Jail seems to agree with you." His scarred smile widens. "I was worried the stress might be too much, given your... delicate condition."

My blood freezes. He knows. Somehow, despite all my precautions, he knows about the pregnancy.

"I don't know what you're talking about."

"Don't you?" He leans forward, and I catch a whiff of the expensive cologne he's always worn. "Four and a half months along, I'd guess. My child, conceived that night after the gala when you were so perfectly obedient."

The words confirm my worst fears. He's not just alive; he's exactly the same manipulative monster he always was. And now he knows about the one thing I've been trying to protect.

"Where is she?" The question bursts out before I can stop it. "Where is Emilie?"

His expression doesn't change, but something flickers in his eyes. "I'm afraid I don't know what you mean."

"My daughter. Our daughter. Who did you give her to?"

"Madeline," he says with that patronizing tone I remember so well, "I think the stress of your situation may be affecting your memory. We don't have a daughter."

The gaslighting is so smooth, so practiced, that for a moment I almost doubt myself. But I remember everything; holding her, feeding her, the way she would light up when she saw me.

"Stop lying. I know you gave her away while we were out that one day. I know—"

"You know what?" His voice remains maddeningly calm. "You're talking about a child that doesn't exist, *ma souris*. There are no birth records, no medical files, no documentation of any kind. Are you sure this isn't some kind of... delusion brought on by trauma?"

The worst part is that he's right about the documentation. Victoria had explained it to me weeks ago, how difficult it was to prove a child had been given away when there was no official record that one had ever been born. Gaspard had been careful, keeping everything off the books, using private doctors who answered only to him.

"I carried her for nine months," I whisper. "I gave birth to her in your house."

"Did you?" He tilts his scarred head. "Because as far as any official record is concerned, you've never been pregnant before the child you're carrying now. Perhaps the isolation, the stress of our... unconventional situation... made you imagine things that weren't there."

My hands tremble as I place them flat on the table. He's rewriting history, making me question my own memories, my own experience. But I remember her weight in my arms, her tiny fingers wrapped around mine, the way she smelled like innocence and hope.

"She was real," I say firmly.

"If you say so." His shrug is dismissive. "Though I do worry about these... episodes you seem to be having. Postpartum psychosis can be quite serious, even when there was no actual pregnancy to trigger it."

The casual cruelty of it takes my breath away. Not only is he denying Emilie's existence, he's suggesting I'm mentally unstable for remembering her. It's psychological torture of the highest order.

I'm tired of his stupid fucking games.

"What do you want?" I ask quietly, doing my best to hide how sick to my stomach he makes me.

His laugh is different now, rougher, probably due to damage from the attack. But the cruelty behind it is unchanged.

"I want my family back, *ma souris*. My wife, my unborn child, and my place in this world that you tried so hard to destroy." His fingers drum against the table. "And fortunately, I'm the only person who can give you what you want."

"Which is?"

"Freedom, of course. You see, I've been thinking during my recovery about what happened that night. About how a gas leak might have caused confusion, disorientation. How someone might have attacked me thinking I was an intruder in my own home."

I stare at him in shock. "You're going to lie."

"I'm going to tell the truth as I see it." His scarred smile doesn't waver. "A traumatic brain injury can affect memory, you know. The doctors have been quite concerned about my recollections of that evening. Very... malleable, they seem to be."

The trap closes around me with perfect precision. He's offering me freedom, but at a price I'm not sure I can pay. And he knows I'm pregnant, which means he has leverage I didn't know he possessed.

"What's the catch?" I ask.

"No catch. I'm simply a forgiving husband who wants his family reunited." He pauses, his damaged gaze dropping to my stomach. "All of his family."

The baby kicks inside me as if sensing the presence of their father, and I have to fight not to react. It's been easy to hide the pregnancy so far; from the weight I lost during those final months with Gaspard, the loose jail uniforms, the fact that I was always small to begin with. Even at almost twenty weeks, I can still pass for someone who's simply gained a little weight. But he sees everything, notices everything.

"I'll be released?" I ask carefully.

"Within twenty-four hours. All charges dropped, record expunged. You'll be free to go wherever you wish." His smile turns predatory. "Though I do hope you'll consider coming home. After all, we have so much to discuss about our future together."

He speaks as if I wouldn't end up right back in jail if I dared not to return 'home' to him. "And if I refuse?"

"Then I'm afraid my memory will return quite clearly. Self-defense is difficult to prove when the victim remembers being attacked without provocation by his unstable wife." He shrugs. "Twenty to life, I believe the prosecutor mentioned? Such a long time behind bars without seeing your child because as you can imagine, I wouldn't want my child tainted by a sick mother's actions."

The room spins around me as the full scope of his manipulation becomes clear. He's using my pregnancy as leverage, my maternal instincts as weapons against me. Either way, he wins; either I return to him willingly, or I lose everything while he plays the victimized husband.

"I need time to think," I say.

"Of course. But not too much time. I'm scheduled to give my statement tomorrow afternoon." He stands slowly, leaning heavily on his cane. "I do hope you'll make the right choice, *ma souris*. For all our sakes."

As he shuffles toward the door, he pauses and looks back at me one last time.

"Oh, and wife? I'm so looking forward to meeting our son."

The door closes behind him with a soft click, leaving me alone with the impossible choice he's presented.

Freedom at the cost of returning to my captor.

Or prison, and losing this baby the way I lost Emilie.

I place both hands over my stomach, feeling the steady flutter of movement within, and realize that no matter what I choose, Gaspard has won again.

Some prisons, I'm learning, have no walls at all.

To Be Continued...
Love Him (Sin and Innocence Part Three)
Coming soon!

Join my reader's list by clicking here to stay up-to-date on new releases, pre-sales, giveaways, events & more. No spam ever!

ABOUT THE AUTHOR

Violet Haze is a big fan of writing and reading romance. The autistic mother of one, she currently spends her days writing, reading, procrastinating, playing violin, & listening to her son play video games she doesn't understand.

For information on other books you can read, including links to ALL the vendors, visit her website:
www.authorviolethaze.com!

Want to contact Violet?
Email her at: violet@authorviolethaze.com
Search for "Author Violet Haze" on Instagram, Facebook, & TikTok!